YOUR *Heart* IS MINE

A Criminal Romance

A NOVEL BY

VIVIAN BLUE

Published by Royalty Publishing House
www.royaltypublishinghouse.com

Contains explicit language & adult themes suitable for ages 16+

CHAPTER ONE

"Come on, Lay! Let me get them earrings. I promise you I won't lose them," pleaded Ew Baby. "You saw I was on fire, and I know you made a few hundred off my run."

"Girl… you tripping! My mama gave me these earrings on my eighteenth birthday, and I'm twenty-two," Lay replied. "She'd kill me if she knew I gave you my earrings to shoot dice."

"But she ain't gon' know, 'cause I ain't gon' lose 'em," whined Ew Baby, trying to assure Lay. They were standing outside the gambling house on McMillian, and Ew Baby was itching to roll those dice one more time to make up the money she'd lost.

"Ew Baby, it's almost six o'clock, and you know we got to get to work," fussed Lay, crossing her arms in front of her. "I don't know about you, but I be tired of getting cursed out by my mama. You know Mama is extra, and she don't care if we're her kids or not."

"But all I need is ten minutes. You know I was on fire, Lay, until that little weasel looking muthafucker jumped in the game. I was licking them niggas," Ew Baby gloated.

"You was killing them," Lay admitted with a hesitant look on her face. "But apparently, your arm got cold because you quickly lost all of your money."

"I got five hundred dollars, but it's $1,500 to get in," Ew Baby whined. "All those niggas that sell dope over on Walton is in this muthafucka now, and they trying to control who's in the game. Those bitch ass niggas hate to see a bitch coming 'cause they know I got them hands!"

"Or trying to set a muthafucka up to get robbed," Lay replied, rolling her eyes.

"*Pleeease*, Lay! Let me get them earrings, and I promise I won't lose them," begged Ew Baby. Lay looked at her best friend of nineteen years and shook her head as she began taking the earrings out of her earlobes. She'd given her earrings to Ew Baby once before and got them right back, so why would tonight be any different?

"Ew Baby, you better not lose my earrings, or I'm gon' beat your ass because my mama's gon' beat mine if she finds out I gave them to you to shoot dice," Lay fussed, handing them to Ew Baby. Ew Baby's eyes glimmered as she clasped her hand around the large diamonds.

"Thanks, sis! I promise I won't lose them!" Ew Baby knocked on the door of the apartment then turned the knob. She walked into the house with Lay in tow. "I'm back, niggas!" shouted Ew Baby. "Y'all better get ready!" she announced, walking over to Big Daddy. He was the one who ran the gambling house for ManMan, and he knew Ew Baby and Lay quite well.

"What's up, Ew Baby?" asked Big Daddy, looking her up and down. "You came over here so we can work something out for you to get back into the game? We can go upstairs real fast and take care of that." He licked his lips suggestively as he smiled at her lustfully.

"Fuuuuck naw!" shouted Ew Baby. "You know better than that! What I look like fucking my mama's ole man?"

"What she don't know won't hurt," he replied. "You know we got a special bond."

"You're a whole pedophile! That's why Ew Baby lives with us now," seethed Lay as she glared at Big Daddy in disgust. "I'm gon' tell my uncles how you talking to her, and you know how they gon' handle that!"

Big Daddy's face quickly turned from a smug ass smile to frown. "You ain't got to be putting them all up in my bid-ness, Lay," Big Daddy retorted.

"And you don't have to talk to my best friend like that!" snapped Lay. "Where ManMan at anyway? Ole flunky ass nigga!"

Big Daddy looked at Lay vehemently. "You got a whole lot of mouth, girl. I bet if yo' mama wasn't Big Lee, you wouldn't be bumping yo' gums like that." Big Daddy smirked.

"It don't matter who my mama is…" Lay frowned, placing her hand on her hip. "I got these hands to back up what I say! And if that don't work, then…" She raised up her shirt, exposing her gun as she tilted her head over to the side and smacked her lips. "Now what else you gotta to say?"

"What's going on?" asked ManMan, walking down the steps. Big Daddy always sat at the bottom of them as a guard, and ManMan heard the exchange between him and the girls. That's what made him come down to see what was going on. Big Daddy was ManMan's uncle, so his job was given to him by default. He wasn't ManMan's favorite person, but he could be quite effective when needed.

"I need to holla at you for a minute." Ew Baby smiled. She perked up her titties and pushed her ass out because she had the biggest crush on ManMan.

"Ah yeah, Ew Baby." ManMan smirked. He looked around her and winked at Lay. "Hey, Layloni."

She threw her hand up and waved nonchalantly at him. She didn't like the way he always lustfully looked at her. It was like he was undressing her with his eyes, and it made her feel uncomfortable. Ew Baby noticed how he was checking out Lay, and she knew Lay didn't like it by the expression on her face.

"Uhhh, ManMan, like I said, I got something I want to holla at you about." Ew Baby smacked her lips.

"Come on. Let's go into the kitchen," ManMan replied, still staring at Lay. "You coming too, Layloni?"

"Unfortunately…" She sighed, rolling her eyes up in her head.

ManMan laughed as he made it to the bottom of the stairs. "Is it that bad?" he asked with a smug smile on his face.

"Yes, it is. I have to be at work in like five minutes, and if I'm late, my mama's gonna cuss my ass out," Lay replied with an attitude.

"Well, let's get to it then. I don't want to make you late for work." ManMan smiled.

They walked into the kitchen so Ew Baby could pawn the earrings to ManMan. He looked over at Lay's ears and noticed she wasn't wearing the ones she normally had on. Ew Baby was doing all the talking, so he figured she'd talked Lay into giving them to her. He cashed Ew Baby out without any problem, but he figured this would be his way to get at Lay and convince her to mess with him. He'd been sweating her for years, but she wouldn't give him any play.

They walked back out of the kitchen, and Ew Baby headed straight to the table. Ew Baby and Lay stood back and watched as they watched a dude name Spud roll until he crapped out. It was Ew Baby's turn to roll, and she was determined to win big. Lay looked over at ManMan as he nodded his head at James, the person who was running the table. He moved everyone back and told Ew Baby it was her turn to roll. He handed her a pair of dice as she threw the money down on the table.

"I'm back, bitch ass niggas! Now let's get ready to dance!" Ew Baby smiled, shaking up the dice. "Kiss these muthafuckas, Lay. We about to get paid in this biotch!" Ew Baby released the dice out of her hand and then rolled them down the table.

"Seven!" shouted James, and everyone went crazy as Ew Baby leaned back and screamed.

"Hot damn!" shouted Ew Baby. "I told you, Lay! I got this!"

James handed Ew Baby the dice. "We got a woman on fire!" he yelled. "What you betting?"

"I'm gon' let it all ride," Ew Baby replied.

"Ew Baby!" shouted Lay. Ew Baby looked at her and smiled her famous gold-toothed smile. She had two golds on her front teeth and one on the bottom to the right.

"Kiss these muthafuckas again, best friend." Ew Baby smiled, holding the dice in front of Lay. "I got this, sis. Trust me!" Lay kissed the dice before Ew Baby shook them up in her hand. She let them go and watched in anticipation as they rolled down the table. The dice landed, but before anyone could see them, James called snake eyes and snatched them up, causing mass hysteria to break out in the house.

"Wait a muthafuckin' minute!" shouted Damon, one of the players sitting around the table. He jumped up out of his seat and started waving his hands in the air.

"Aye… Aye… Aye!" shouted Ew Baby. "How you gon' call the dice then snatch them up before anyone gets to see them?"

Lay's head fell into her chest as Ew Baby continued to go off on James. "My mama's gon' kill me!" cried Lay, shaking her head from side to side. "I done fucked up big time!"

CHAPTER TWO

"Y'all better have a good ass reason why y'all twenty minutes late!" fussed Big Lee, coming from around the bar.

"Mama, let me explain," Lay stammered, tying her apron around her waist. "We were out in North County at the Walmart, picking up our cleaning supplies and other odds and ends."

"Why didn't you go around to the house and get stuff out of my pantry?" Big Lee questioned, sounding annoyed. "You know I always tell you to go get what you need out of there."

"I know, Mama, but sometimes, I try to be independent," Lay replied. Big Lee smiled at her baby because she was so proud of her. In a few months, she would be graduating from St. Louis University with her Bachelors in Business and Finance. Big Lee had a big surprise for her baby girl after she crossed that stage, and she couldn't wait to give it to her.

"It was more my fault, Mama," Ew Baby admitted. "I was the one slow dragging through the store." Big Lee looked at Ew Baby, her foster daughter. She and Lay had been best friends since they were three years old, when she and her mama, Patricia, moved on the block. Patricia was an undercover dope fiend, but her shit got raggedy when her man got locked up, who just so happened to be married to Big Lee.

See, Ew Baby was Cecil's daughter, but no one knew except Big Lee, the brothers, and Patricia. Ew Baby's real name was Cecilia Antoinette Jones, and when the state was about to take Ew Baby from Patricia, Cecil begged Big Lee to take her so she wouldn't go to a foster home. Big Lee agreed on the condition that no one told Ew Baby or Layloni that Cecil was Ew Baby's daddy. Big Lee had a secret of her own about Lay's paternity, but her infidelities would have been exposed, and that was a can of worms that she didn't want to open. However, this was the driving force that made Big Lee get their marriage annulled.

"What am I going to do with you, Ew Baby?" Big Lee fussed. "Your ass is always dragging through this muthafucka, but you better make sure those grades are poppin' this semester! I'm not paying good money for your ass to go to cosmetology school, only for you to fuck it off!"

"Yes, ma'am," Ew Baby replied. "I'm doing much better since I got a study partner."

"That's good," Big Lee replied. She settled on her usual seat at the bar while Lay wiped it down like she did every day before she started her shift. She liked to sit in the corner, where she could watch everything that was going on. There was another side to the lounge with a dance floor and tables set out around the space. She had video cameras set up all around the lounge, where she would watch them behind the bar. She wanted to see who was coming in and out of her lounge just in case some shit might pop off. There was a room upstairs where you could shoot pool, throw darts, or have a private party.

Also, Big Lee owned the apartments next door to the lounge, and you could get into the one that was connected to the building through a side door. That was considered the clubhouse apartment for the brothers when they got too drunk or were sneaking around on their women. Big Lee was very protective of her six brothers, and she had beaten up plenty of women and lost a lot of friends over them.

Whisper, Big Lee's driver and right-hand man, came through the door with his cocky demeanor. He smiled when he saw his favorite goddaughter behind the bar, and it looked like she was barely working. Whisper, a.k.a. Jamal Thompson, was best friends with Ralph and Rico, Big Lee's twin brothers. He grew up around the corner from the Wilson family and was a permanent fixture in their household. He had a little brother, Josh, who was doing life in prison plus a hundred years for a double murder. He and Whisper were still very close even though Josh would never see the streets again.

"What's up, princess?" Whisper called out. He noticed she had a sad look on her face and wondered what that was about.

"Just the person I needed to see!" Lay shouted, perking up when she saw her godfather approaching. Whisper smiled, showing all six of his gold teeth as he made his way to the bar. Normally, he'd have his bottom grill in that was covered with diamonds. The top gold teeth were permanently in his mouth, but he only put the bottom grill in when he wanted to stunt. Lay and Ew Baby were secretly infatuated and in love with Whisper because he was fine as hell to them. His complexion was caramel brown, and he had strong, chiseled features. His light-brown bedroom eyes made women weak at the knees, with a broad nose and mouth that was surrounded by a full beard and mustache that was well kept. It was obvious that he really cared about his appearance, because he was always put together. Whisper had his low Caesar cut lined and faded with waves that flowed like the ocean. All the ladies wanted to get a taste of this handsome thug, but he was no easy target to get to. He stood about five feet eleven and was cocky and bow legged. His muscles rippled through his upper chest and back, and when he wore tank tops, it absolutely drove the women crazy.

"What's the word?" Whisper asked. Lay looked over at her mother nervously.

"I can't talk right now," Lay stuttered, continuing to stare over at her mother. "Mama's sitting right there, and I don't want her to hear."

"Have somebody been fucking with you?" Whisper asked and frowned.

"No, Whisper," Lay replied, smiling. She loved it when he got overprotective about her. It made her feel special and safe. "But I am in a bit of a jam."

Whisper raised an eyebrow at his goddaughter because he didn't like her response.

"You must need some money," he replied, smirking.

"Not quite," she replied. "But I'll talk to you in a minute. You better go check in 'cause I see how mama's looking over here at us."

Whisper smiled as he looked up at Big Lee, and their eyes met. Whisper winked and blew a kiss at her, and Big Lee frowned as she looked around the bar. Big Lee got up and walked away because she didn't feel like playing with Whisper.

“You better quit playing with her,” Ew Baby mentioned then smirked, sliding up on the side of Whisper. “Mama’s gonna fuck you up about your messiness!”

Whisper looked down at Ew Baby and grinned. “Let me worry about Ann, lil’ mama.” Whisper laughed. “I got this under control.” Ew Baby looked over at Lay, and they both turned their lips up at the same time.

“You ain’t got nothing, Whisper.” Ew Baby scoffed. “‘Cause we all know Mama’s running things.”

Whisper looked at Ew Baby and shook his head because he knew no matter what he said to them, they were always going to ride with Big Lee. “Now what is it you want to talk to me about?” Whisper asked, studying his goddaughter. He sat down at the bar as she put a glass of ice in front of him. She pulled a Kiwi Strawberry Mystic out of the cooler and opened it before pouring it into the glass.

“Whisper, you have to promise that you won’t tell my mama,” Lay pleaded, looking around the bar. KeKe, the head bartender, walked by, eyeing them as she leaned over to grab a beer.

“Hey, Whisper,” KeKe said coyly.

“Hey, KeKe,” Whisper replied and smiled. She blushed as she stared back at him and licked her lips seductively.

“Would you be smiling that hard if my mama was sitting right here?” asked Lay with a bit of an attitude. KeKe’s face instantly dropped, and she glared over at Lay.

“Damn, Lay! Can’t nobody speak to Whisper?” asked KeKe, sarcastically.

"Ain't nobody said nothing about speaking. I'm talking about how you showing him all of your teeth with that big ass smile," Lay shot back. "Y'all hoes know my mama don't play when it comes to Whisper. She told y'all that he was off limits, and she'll fuck one of y'all up if she catches any of you up in his face!"

KeKe looked at Lay coyly as she remembered her boss's exact words.

"Point taken, niece. So I'm about to carry my ass back down to the other end of the bar with John and line me up a date for tonight."

Lay and Whisper laughed as KeKe walked down to the other end of the bar. Nobody messed with Big Lee, because she was the last person that you wanted to cross.

"Now what's up, lil' mama, before Ann comes back upstairs?" Whisper asked curiously.

Lay took a deep breath because she knew Whisper was getting ready to go off on her.

"I need to borrow your earrings Mama bought you," Lay blurted out.

"Where are your earrings?" asked Whisper, looking at Lay with a raised eyebrow.

"I don't want to get into all of that. Can you do that for me?" Lay begged.

"I can do it for you, but you need to offer up an explanation, lil' mama," Whisper replied and smirked.

Lay dropped her head then brought it back up, resting her eyes on

Whisper. Ew Baby walked by and noticed Whisper and Lay talking, so she instantly turned back around and walked the other way.

"Me and Ew Baby was around on McMillian at ManMan's house…"

"Haven't I told y'all asses to stay out of there!" snapped Whisper, frowning. "That place ain't right, and it's no place for you and Ew Baby!"

"I tried to stop her, Whisper, but once she gets to shooting dice, it's hard to get her to stop," Lay explained. "Anyway, she had lost most of her money, and she had five hundred dollars left. Them dudes off Walton was up in there, so they had raised the pot to $1,500 to get in the game. Ew Baby begged me to give her my earrings to pawn to ManMan. She promised not to lose them, and I had to back her up. She pawned them to ManMan for a grand and used the money to get back in the game. She rolled a seven on her first roll and won the money back, but we both know Ew Baby wasn't gon' stop there. She was on fire, Whisper; that's why I rolled with her. She's my best friend, my sister, and I just couldn't say no."

"How far in was she before she lost?" asked Whisper frankly.

"That's the thing! On her second roll, James called snake eyes then snatched up the dice before anyone could see them! Everyone was pissed off, and the house went crazy!" Lay explained. "I saw ManMan nod his head at James before Ew Baby rolled, so I knew something fishy was going on."

"Sounds like he set you girls up," Whisper replied. "But I'm not going to help you. You're always letting Ew Baby get you jammed up in something, and one day, she's going to get you into something that you can't get out of."

"You sound like my mama, Whisper, but you're my Godfather! Therefore, you're supposed to help me get out of jams, especially, when my mama's concerned," whined Lay. "She's going to be hella upset, not only because I let Ew Baby lose my earrings, but 'cause she told me to stay out of ManMan's place because he doesn't run a fair game." Lay looked disappointed as she grabbed her purse from up under the counter. Whisper watched his goddaughter as she came from around the bar.

"Where you going, lil' girl?" Whisper asked nonchalantly.

"To smoke a blunt. I need to figure out something so I can go get my earrings," Lay replied. Whisper watched her go to the rear of the lounge then walk out the back door. He wanted to help her, but she had to learn this hard lesson on her own.

CHAPTER THREE

Big Lee, Whisper, and five of her brothers—Deacon, Rico, Ralph, Cam, and Ax—were down in the basement of the lounge, along with Teke, a dope fiend that worked for Big Lee. He did odd jobs around the lounge and her other properties; plus, he was Big Lee's self-proclaimed protector. He was in charge of collecting and throwing away all the trash at the lounge, storefronts, the convenience store, and garage. Also, he cleaned up the lounge, the front of the rental properties, and the boarding house he ran for Big Lee, located next door to the lounge. Teke was Big Lee's eyes and ears around the hood. She looked out for him and took damn good care of him, and because of that, he kept his ears to the ground for her. He even had a nice van that she bought to help him get around to do his job. Big Lee understood if you treated the people who worked for you like family, their loyalty would be forever in your favor.

"C-c-come on, Big Lee," Sherman stuttered. "I promise you! I'm sorry, and it won't happen again!"

"I know it's not going to happen again, because I'm about to cut off your fingers to make sure it doesn't!" Big Lee snapped. "The only reason I'm not going to kill you is because I know your mama, and it would destroy her if I killed your pathetic ass!"

"Fuck that shit, Big Lee!" Deacon shouted. "Kill that nigga dead! He's been fucking with the church's money, several times I might add, and we keep sparing this son of a bitch 'cause of his mammy!"

Deacon, forty-five and the second oldest brother, was known as the mediator of the Wilson crew. He ran the convenience store that was across the street from the lounge. They both sat on opposite corners of Martin Luther King Drive and Billups Avenue, along with a strip mall that had four storefronts that Big Lee owned. One housed a restaurant ran by Big Lee's best friend Jasmine, a.k.a. Jazzy, who was married to Deacon, and they have three kids: Mary at nineteen, Joseph at sixteen, and Deacon Jr. at eleven.

"Ann about to fuck that nigga up!" Ralph teased, laughing.

"I don't know why he even thought to fuck with big sis," Rico added. "We all know her ass is crazy! She'll fuck one of us up for taking something from her ass, and we're her brothers!"

"Remember, she fucked me up when I borrowed her car that one time," Ralph reminisced. Big Lee cut her eyes at him because he wrecked her car that night.

Ralph and Rico were the only set of twins that their parents had out of their children. They were under Big Lee, and the fraternal twins were thirty-seven years old. Neither one of them were married, but they both had kids. Ralph had a common-law wife, Shai, and they'd been together since they were sixteen years old. They had a set of girl twins, Winter and Autumn, who were sixteen years old. Rico had a baby mama, Chrissy, and they had a son, Suave, who was seventeen years old. Chrissy felt that Ralph was too much of a hoe, so they didn't get along. Ralph and Rico occupied the second storefront of Big Lee's property and ran the family drycleaners. They were the coolest out of the Wilson crew because everyone always wanted them around.

"I'll take care of him," Ax insisted, pulling his gun out of his waistband. He took it off safety and pulled back the slide, placing a round in the chamber.

"Yeah, sis, let Ax pop that nigga up and get it over with," Cam agreed. "I know it's some bitches upstairs ready to make my acquaintance, and this shit is taking too damn long!"

The youngest of the Wilson crew, Cameron, a.k.a. Cam at twenty-eight, and Axel, a.k.a. Ax at twenty-five, were the hotheads. They ran a garage that housed a mechanic, an auto body shop, and a car wash all in one. It sat on a lot behind the convenience store, but it was diagonal from the lounge. Big Lee sent them to Ranken as well to get their degrees in automotive and auto bodywork. Neither one of them had children, but Cam had been married to his high-school sweetheart, Tamara, for three years, while Ax was young, single, and liked to mingle.

"Put that thing away, Ax!" Big Lee snapped. "Muthafuckas upstairs will hear your banger go off. Besides, death is too good for this petty ass nigga, and like I said, I can't do that to his mother. She's like an aunt to us, so this muthafucka's gon' have to suffer by becoming handicapped. We'll see how much he can steal with nubs!" Teke held Sherman's hand as he lifted the meat cleaver, and everyone stared in anticipation to what was about to happen. *Wham...* went the meat cleaver, hitting the piece of tree stub Big Lee had brought to the basement for this purpose. Teke missed Sherman's hand by a mile, and this totally pissed Big Lee off!

"You must be a blind as a muthafucka to miss all four of his fingers!" Deacon shouted. "'Cause you missed them shits by a mile!" Big Lee hit her cigar as she glared over at Teke.

"I gave your ass a fix before we came to do this," Big Lee reminded him. "Your hands should be steady as a muthafucka, and you better not miss this time, or Ax is going to do both of you, and I don't give a fuck about people hearing the shots!"

Ax looked at Teke with a serious expression then smiled. He was a hothead and crazy as fuck, so Teke didn't want to take his chances with him.

"O-o-okay, Big Lee," Teke stuttered, nervously. "My eyes weren't in focus." He wiped both of them in support of his lie because he'd fucked up by missing his mark.

Sherman looked up at Big Lee and Deacon, petrified as Whisper and Cam laughed hysterically behind them. Big Lee turned around and looked at both of them disapprovingly, then she turned her attention back to Sherman, who was sweating profusely. Teke raised the meat cleaver again as he held Sherman's hand steadily. He brought the heavy blade down hard, but missed his fingers again. However, this time Sherman had moved it out of the way, preventing Teke from cutting them off. By this time, Big Lee was super pissed because she felt like too many games were being played at the wrong time.

"Hold this!" she snapped, handing Deacon her cigar. "Hold his hand down, Teke!" Teke did what she asked and grabbed Sherman's arm and fingers. Big Lee picked up a hammer, and drove a nail straight through Sherman's hand. He bellowed out in pain as blood began to seep all over the tree stump.

"I bet your bitch ass ain't gon' move now!" Deacon teased, handing Big Lee her Cuban back.

"Now hurry up and cut that muthafucka's fingers off!" Big Lee snapped in frustration. Teke held up the meat cleaver one last time and came down on Sherman's fingers, cutting all four of them clean off. They all sporadically rolled across the tree stump as all the men made an 'uhhh' sound.

"I hope you're left handed," Teke joked while Big Lee fired up the big cigar that she'd been puffing on. She pulled on it hard as she stared, satisfied that the job had been done.

"Give him a shot, Teke, so he won't go into shock," Big Lee ordered. Teke grabbed a jar of white liquid off the shelf. "That's some of Mississippi's finest moonshine. White Lightening is what they call it. I'm gon' give you a few shots of it because I'm going to burn all your nubs with this cigar, and it's going to hurt like hell! I advise you to go to the hospital when we finish, and I'm sure you know how to lie about what happened. Especially since you always come to us with a bullshit story when you're short." Teke gave Sherman a double shot, and he took it straight down like a champ.

"You vicious as a muthafucka, big sis." Ax laughed.

"What did Mama do when you called yourself stealing candy out of the corner store?" Big Lee asked, placing the cigar on Sherman's finger. He screamed as his flesh began to sizzle against the cherry of the cigar.

"She whooped my hands until they were red as fire," Ax replied, taking a hit of the moonshine. He passed it over to Whisper, but he declined after he got a whiff of the smell.

"I don't see how y'all drink that shit!" Whisper frowned.

"Get my jar and put a little juice in it, Teke," Big Lee ordered as she burned the third finger. Teke walked over to the walk-in freezer and came out with a large pickle jar. He walked over to the sink and put a little of a mixture that contained siloxane, a semifluorinated alkane, and a hydrofluoroether in side of it. Deacon was a master at chemistry and got a chemical engineering degree from Mizzou when he was the ripe age of twenty-three. He was able to look up and order chemicals that the average person wouldn't have access too, because he did some freelance work for a biochemical company when he felt like it. Teke walked over to the table where the tree stump sat and began picking up Sherman's fingers, putting them in the jar.

"Deacon, call Craig and tell him we got a clean-up. He can come pick up this tree stump and chop it down to firewood for the pit," Big Lee instructed, burning Sherman's last finger. "You see that jar right there? That's my collection of fingers from muthafuckas like you that think you can steal from the Wilsons. I got 151 fingers in there, and your four makes 155. You ain't the first muthafucka who thought it was alright to steal from us, and you definitely won't be the last. But you, Sherman, my boy, will think long and hard before you do the shit again!"

"I lost two of mines, taking shit from Big Lee," Teke bragged, holding up his left hand. "She showed mercy on me when she should have killed me dead. Big Lee knew I was geek'd up, but she made me pay for my mistake."

"Get your story telling ass over here and clean up this table! This meat cleaver, hammer, and nail needs to be sanitized properly. I don't want to see a drop of blood when I come back down here," Big Lee fussed.

Ax laughed as he walked up the steps because he knew his big sister was no joke! She was from the old school, and she'd rather administer torture before killing you, whereas Ax would just kill you quickly.

Craig came downstairs with a trash can and a lid in his hands. He looked around the room as Teke pulled the nail out of Sherman's hand with a pair of pliers. Craig had seen this scene far too many times and wondered when would people learn about stealing from his little sister. He got to the bottom of the steps and smiled when Sherman cried out in excruciating pain.

Craig was the eldest of the Wilson children. He was forty-eight years old and married to his high-school sweetheart, Val. They had three adult sons, Craig Jr. who was thirty, Travis at twenty-five, and Malcolm was twenty-three. Craig was over the maintenance department that took care of all the rental properties and businesses that Big Lee owned. He and his sons cleaned, cut grass, fixed leaks, and took care of extra things that needed to be handled. Big Lee paid for all of them to go to Ranken Technical College to learn heating and cooling and electrical and plumbing just like their father. The boys hoped to one day open their own construction company, and their aunt would have no problem helping them achieve their dream.

"What's going on?" Craig called out, walking up on Big Lee. He gave his little sister a kiss on the cheek as he smiled at her finger jar. "Some stupid muthafuckas been stealing again, huh?"

"You already know." Big Lee scoffed, screwing the top on the jar. She went over to the walk-in freezer as Craig picked up the tree stump and put it in the trash can. Whisper followed Big Lee into the freezer as she put the jar in the very back on the top shelf. He walked up on her and wrapped his arms around her thick waist. Big Lee was a sexy, thick chick that was sixteen in the waist and cute in the face.

"Why did you get up and leave so early this morning?" asked Big Lee with a hint of an attitude. "I planned on making you a little breakfast in bed, but you spoiled my plans."

Whisper kissed her on neck as he squeezed her tightly. "Amber showed up at my house this morning, so I slid out the back door and pretended I didn't hear the phone ringing," Whisper explained.

"I guess it's convenient for you since our backyards are connected," Big Lee mentioned, turning around to face him. "I don't know why you didn't leave that bitch standing out there. She ain't even your style no way." Big Lee cut her eyes at Whisper, and he smiled at his boo 'cause her jealousy began to show. They'd messed around for years but never made it official.

She was two years older than him, and he was the same age as Ralph and Rico. They were so used to sneaking around that their relationship remained in the background no matter who they decided to date. Her twin brothers were the reason she and Whisper began creeping around. He used to come over to hang out with them, but somehow, he always ended up in Big Lee's room. There was one point when everyone thought that Big Lee and Whisper were going to be a couple, but Cecil somehow slid in and brainwashed Big Lee, causing her to distance herself from Whisper.

When Cecil got locked up, Whisper was right there to hold Big Lee down. Cecil was always jealous of Whisper and Big Lee's relationship because she trusted Whisper more than she did him, and the brothers always had Whisper watching over Big Lee to protect her. That's why he was her driver when none of the brothers were available to take her where she needed to go, so it was a no brainer that when she came into her money, she hired him to be her personal bodyguard.

"Ms. Wilson, you know you come first in my life," Whisper cooed, kissing her lips. "But you are a married woman."

"And the nigga is in prison," she replied. "Would you believe me if I told you our marriage wasn't valid."

Whisper looked at her strangely. "You'd have to show me some paperwork to prove it to me," Whisper replied. "But you know I don't give a fuck no way! You'll always be mine, with or without that piece of paper."

Big Lee smiled as she wrapped her arms around Whisper's neck and kissed him passionately. Those words that he spoke were music to her ears, and she felt that no matter what, Whisper would always be hers as well.

CHAPTER FOUR

"Good morning," said Big Lee, getting in the car.

"Good morning, baby," Whisper replied and smiled. He leaned over and gave her a kiss on the lips, but she turned her head, and it landed on her cheek. Big Lee had a bit of an attitude because Whisper didn't spend the night with her last night, and he picked up on it by her actions.

"We need to make our rounds before I go to the office. I want to pick up the drops early because I don't want people to clock our schedule. It's the fifteenth of the month, and I need to pick up my rent money," Big Lee explained. Whisper could tell something was wrong because she was being real short and direct this morning.

"Whatever you want, Ann," Whisper replied, pulling out of the driveway.

Big Lee owned a big house in the Central West End, and Whisper stayed directly behind the house, in her carriage house apartment, when Big Lee wanted to stay over at that house. She owned a lot of properties around the city, so she always kept him close to her. Whisper was the true love of her life, and she had a soft spot in her heart for him.

There were times when she wished she'd just told Whisper how she felt instead of choosing Cecil. However, Whisper never asked or made his feelings known, so she went with Cecil, the lousy muthafucka. The chatter was getting louder about some chick he messed with on the northside named Angie. Apparently, Cecil had been taking care of her for the past few years. She had gone to visit him and smuggled some contraband up in the penitentiary as a favor from Cecil's celly. After that visit, Cecil declared Angie as his gal, and they'd been rocking together ever since. Cecil hooked her up with his brother, and Angie was moving and grooving for Cecil behind Big Lee's back.

"What's on your mind, Ann?" Whisper asked nonchalantly. "I can tell something's wrong with you."

"I talked to Cecil's ass before I came out the house," Big Lee replied, sounding irritated. "He wants me to come up there to visit him on Sunday, but I'm not feeling it."

"So don't go," Whisper replied. "I don't know why you messed with his weak ass in the first place. He was never really into you; it was all about your status."

Big Lee cut her eyes at Whisper. "Damn, thanks a lot," she replied, sarcastically.

"You know what I mean, baby," Whisper replied, grabbing her hand. He kissed the back of it, trying to ease things over.

Big Lee looked at him, and her face softened. Whisper smiled as he admired her cocoa-colored skin, fat cheeks, button nose, and big, pretty eyes. He loved her thick thighs, big hips, fat ass, and big breasts. She didn't have any stomach, because she worked out with a personal trainer four times a week. If she felt motivated, she and Whisper would go out for walks early in the morning around the neighborhood. She liked to observe their hood when it was supposed to be at rest. She knew the bad element was on their way to bed, while the hard-working, honest people were getting ready to go to work.

"I know what you mean," she replied. "I don't know how I got tied up with that clown either. Maybe I was waiting on a certain somebody, but they never stepped to me, so I went with the one who was checking for me."

Whisper looked over at Big Lee because he knew she was talking about him. There was an awkward silence, then Big Lee's phone went off.

"Is it him again?" Whisper asked and frowned.

"Yeah, it's him," Big Lee replied.

"Just don't answer the phone, Ann. Let it go to voicemail." Whisper scoffed. Big Lee looked over at Whisper with a smile on her face.

"Why does it even matter to you? You got your little girlfriend, Amber, who by the way, ain't your type. All she does is complain about shit, and I don't like the way she talks down to you. She ain't got shit, so how she gon' turn her nose up at us. I could buy that two-dollar hoe ten times over then come back and buy her ten more times," Big Lee fussed. Whisper laughed as his lover's fangs came out viciously because he loved when Big Lee showed him just how much she cared. All he wanted was to be with her, but things were a bit complicated, and he was just waiting for the right time.

"Don't you start that shit, Ann! You're so jealous right now," Whisper teased.

"I ain't jealous," she replied, turning up her lips. She reached into her purse and pulled out a cigarette. "Can you go pick up the Benz from the dealer and take it over to the garage to get it detailed. I'm getting tired of riding in this car."

"What's wrong with my car?" Whisper asked. He had a black Impala SS with black-on-black rims and presidential tinted windows.

"Ain't nothing wrong with your car, Whisper. I just think you should be riding something better," she replied. "You have two other cars, so why you always driving this one?"

"I'm happy with this car. This was the first car I bought that wasn't a bucket," Whisper replied, and Big Lee started laughing.

"I remember how we used to pile up in that Regal you had and go skating on Saturday nights at Saints," Big Lee reminisced.

"Those were the days," Whisper agreed. "There used to be damn near ten of us piled in that joint." They both laughed at the memory. Big Lee's phone began to ring again, so she looked down and saw it was Cecil.

"He's going to call until I answer." Big Lee sighed with a weary look on her face. Whisper grabbed her phone out her hand and threw it behind him in the backseat.

"Why did you do that?" Big Lee seethed then frowned.

"Because you're with me, and this is our time we spend together every day," Whisper replied, annoyed. "And he's not about to fuck it up! You're already in a bad mood so that fucks up the flow of the day. I should have turned back around and took you back in the house. If I fucked you real good and sucked that pussy right, it would have put a smile on your face for the rest of the day."

Big Lee smirked as she listened to Whisper talk shit to her. She loved how he made her feel, and he too always got defensive and jealous whenever Cecil was brought up or called. "Naw I'm good," Big Lee said, cutting her eyes at him. "You was with Amber last night so that's like getting sloppy seconds." She side eyed him because she knew that was a blow to his ego. She knew she didn't have room to be that way toward him, but her heart was with Whisper, and she needed to figure out what to do about it.

"Don't get fucked up, you hear me?" Whisper replied. "'Cause the way I see it, Amber's the one who's been getting the sloppy seconds!"

****

"Hello."

"You have a collect call from a correctional facility..."

Lay rolled her eyes as the recording went on. The only time her daddy called her phone was when he couldn't find her mama. Occasionally, he would just call to see how she was doing, but Lay felt like he really wasn't interested. Lay didn't look like him at all and had an uncanny resemblance to Whisper. She has her mother's skin tone and had the slender build Big Lee had when she was a teenager, but Lay had her own look to her that no one could explain. She wasn't well-endowed like her mother in the breast and butt area, but she wasn't short stopping either. Deacon said she looked just like Whisper, but everyone shot that down quickly, saying he was trying to start some shit. However, Lay began to notice some similarities between her and Whisper, like how they smiled alike, and her eyes were light brown like his. Big Lee always told her daughter that Whisper got on her nerves while she was pregnant and that's why Lay looked so much like him.

"Hi, Daddy," said Lay as she made a right onto MLK.

"Hey, Lay," Cecil replied. "How you doing?"

"I'm fine," Lay replied dryly.

"Your mama tells me you're about to graduate from college. I'm proud of you," said Cecil happily.

"Thank you. She told me you're getting out soon, so, maybe you'll be able to make it to the graduation," she replied.

"I'm hoping, baby girl. They say I'm getting out in May, so I have four more months to go," Cecil explained.

"You'll be home in time for the warm weather. It's cold as hell out here today," Lay fussed. "I've been over winter since it arrived."

"Yeah, it's cold as a muthafucka up here in Bonne Terre too." There was brief moment of silence. "You around your mama?" Cecil asked.

"Nope. I just got out of class," Lay replied, rolling her eyes. "Did you call both of her phones?"

"Yeah, but she didn't answer," he replied. Lay looked at the clock.

"You know what? She's probably out making her rounds; it's Friday. She likes to do it early because Happy Hour is off the chain on Fridays. She cooks for everyone and puts out a big spread of food for all of her employees and customers," Lay explained.

"How much money do she be spending doing all of that shit?" Cecil asked with an attitude. Lay frowned as she got an instant attitude.

"Why does it matter? It's her money," Lay replied sarcastically.

"Yeah, it's her money, but them niggas out there eating off her and mooching," he replied.

"And what are you doing, Daddy?" she asked smugly. "You're in jail, and I know she puts about a grand on your books every month."

"You better watch your tone, little girl," Cecil snapped with an attitude. "I'm still your daddy, and you ain't too grown to get a whooping." Lay held the phone for a second and counted to ten. She hated this dude and wished he'd disappear.

"I ain't around Mama, so I'm gon' tell her you called," Lay blurted out. "Do you have a message you want me to relay?"

"Naw, I just talked to her about an hour ago," he replied. Lay rolled her eyes in her head because, what was the purpose of this call?

"Is that nigga Whisper riding her around?" asked Cecil curiously.

"My godfather always rides Mama around. He's her bodyguard," Lay replied, sarcastically.

"Well, that shit's gon' change when I get home. Ain't no other nigga gon' be riding my wife around," Cecil declared.

"I don't know how Mama's gonna feel about that," Lay replied. "But I know my uncles aren't going to go along with it."

Cecil held the phone for a minute, pissed. He forgot about how much influence all Big Lee's brothers had over her, and that drove him crazy. "I'm about to go, Lay. You stay up," Cecil offered.

"You too," Lay replied and hung up abruptly just in case he wanted to say something else. She was over the call when it first came through, and she hoped that his ass wouldn't call again.

Lay hit her call log and hit her mother's number. She let the phone ring as she pulled up in front of her apartment and noticed Whisper's car parked in front of her uncle Ralph's house, which was two doors down from her apartment. Big Lee owned a four-family flat and a twelve-family across from each other on Aldine Avenue. Deacon lived in the house they grew up in on the corner of Billups Avenue and Aldine Avenue with his wife. His oldest two boys were away at college, and Deac Jr. was barely at home. He spent a lot of time around the corner over his uncle Rico's house with his cousin Suave. The children hung out with one another like they were brothers and sisters, and all the Wilson clan were tight!

"Hello," said Big Lee, sounding winded.

"Mama! Why you sound like that?" Lay asked, concerned.

"Do you really want me to answer that question?" Big Lee replied.

"You over Uncle Ralph's house?"

"I might be," she replied. "What's up with the line of questioning? You sound like your damn daddy."

"That's why I'm calling," Lay replied. "He just called me looking for you."

Big Lee started laughing. "You should have told his ass I was busy," she replied. "Boy, stop! I'm talking to our daughter."

"Mama, you play too much! I'll talk to you later." Lay giggled. Big Lee laughed as Whisper continued to suck on her nipple. "Alright, baby girl, I'll see you later." Lay hung up the phone, shaking her head at Cecil's ass.

"My mama plays too much!" Lay mumbled aloud. She knew that man Cecil would flip his lid if he heard Big Lee call Whisper her daddy, but that wasn't the first time that she'd heard that statement.

CHAPTER FIVE

It was five o'clock, and Happy Hour was in full swing on this Friday evening. Big Lee had put out her normal spread of catfish, whiting, tilapia, buffalo, catfish nuggets, and chicken wings. The side dishes she had to accompany the protein were spaghetti, fettuccine with broccoli, baked beans, green beans, coleslaw, potato salad, and tossed salad, with pickles, onions, and cha cha on the side. And for dessert, there was 7 Up pound cake, buttermilk pound cake, chocolate marble strawberry pound cake, apple pie, peach cobbler, and an assortment of cookies. Big Lee did this every Friday for all her employees as a way to say thank you for your service. They'd come to the bar to pick up their checks and get something to eat as well. If they had to come get their checks early, they would go by the office and get them from her personal assistant, Debbie.

"You in a good mood this evening, boss lady," said KeKe, smiling at Big Lee.

"I got me some this afternoon, so everything is right in the world." Big Lee winked.

"Are you still messing with that young dude that's been hanging around for the past few months?" asked KeKe nosily.

"Yeap," Big Lee replied. "I was with him earlier." She was lying because Whisper was the one all up in them guts. KeKe had a big mouth, and she was the one who told Cecil that she and Whisper were messing around, so she didn't want to risk having to fuck KeKe up again.

"What you gon' do when Cecil come home?" KeKe asked.

Big Lee looked over at her smugly. "The same damn thing I've been doing," Big Lee replied. "Cecil don't run nothing over here, and we both know he got a problem with keeping his dick in his pants."

"Speaking of can't keep his dick in his pants… Girl, why did Cam come in here last night with some girl that looked like she was straight from Hoe's Island?" asked KeKe, rolling her eyes. Big Lee fell out laughing at her friend. She'd known KeKe, a.k.a. Kendra, for many, many years because she grew up across Martin Luther King Dr. on Evans. KeKe graduated from Sumner a year before Big Lee, so they knew all the same people.

"Well, you know Cam's young, and he has money. He can be very flashy, especially when he's out with Axel," Big Lee replied. "I just hope that Tamara doesn't catch him."

"That Ax is a mess," KeKe replied. "Do you know he told me he'd pour Sweet Baby Ray's barbecue sauce all over my pussy and eat it off the bone!"

Big Lee laughed as she thought about her baby brother because that was something Deacon would say to a woman. "Was he drunk, girl?" Big Lee asked, tickled.

"You know he was," KeKe replied. "And he fucked the shit out of my old ass last night!"

Big Lee shook her head as KeKe fell out laughing. "You done just about fucked all of my brothers, haven't you?" Big Lee asked, confused. KeKe looked at her shamefully.

"I hang my head in shame because the answer is yes. The only brothers I haven't had sex with are Craig and Cam. I did Ralph and Rico at the same time on the pool table upstairs on a late night one time—"

"KeKe, I don't want to hear anymore," Big Lee hissed as Ew Baby walked up to her. "What's the matter with you? Why your face all drawn up?"

"I just came from around the corner visiting my sisters and brother. It's a damn shame how that house looked," Ew Baby fussed. "Patricia needs her a—I mean, butt beat!"

"That's why you're with me," Big Lee replied. "Yo' mama has always been trifling like that. I'm just glad my baby girl not gon' turn out like her." Big Lee caressed the side of Ew Baby's face.

"That's right, Mama! I don't have time to be a dope fiend," Ew Baby declared. "There's money to be made and niggas to be played!"

"That's right!" Big Lee smiled. "Now go clock in and get your ass over there on the floor and wait those tables."

Ew Baby laughed as she pushed Big Lee on the arm. She leaned over and kissed Big Lee on cheek. "KeKe, my mama crazy ain't she?" Ew Baby asked, walking off to go clock in.

"It's beautiful how you accepted her into your family. I don't know if I could have taken my old man's kid in." KeKe scoffed.

Big Lee looked over at her strangely. "Huh?" Big Lee called out with a frown on her face.

"Girl, you know me and Deacon got our thing going on, on the low, and sometimes when he's been sipping, and I fucked him real good, he likes to pillow talk," KeKe confessed. "And one day, you was upset about something Cecil had done, and it pissed your big brother off. That's how it came out that Ew Baby was Cecil's daughter."

Big Lee was hot! This bitch had one of the biggest mouths in the hood, and her Chatty Charles ass brother done told her business, which was a direct violation. Big Lee smiled coyly at KeKe, but her flesh was burning underneath her skin.

"I couldn't stand by and let Ew Baby go to a foster home. Lay begged and cried for me to let that girl stay with us, and I just couldn't say no to my baby," Big Lee explained. "Even if Ew Baby wasn't Cecil's daughter, I would have still taken her in."

"I know, Big Lee," KeKe replied. "Because you take care of everybody."

"I guess," Big Lee replied nonchalantly. That's what she felt like it was her job to do, and God made sure that she was able to provide for her loved ones.

****

Deacon walked into the lounge, ready for a drink. It had been a long day, and Fridays were the best day of the week. He sat down at the bar, placing his phone and a pack of cigarettes on the counter. KeKe walked up to him and smiled before she placed his usual in front of him.

"Deacon John Wilson!"

Deacon hunched down and turned around slowly. He knew there was going to be trouble whenever his sister called his name like that. "What's up, Ann?" Deacon asked, trying not to start any shit.

"Why did you tell that big mouth heffa my business?" Big Lee asked, walking up to him with an attitude. She put her hands on her hips because she was waiting for his excuse.

"What you talking about, girl?" Deacon asked, frowning. "I ain't told nobody shit!"

"You lying, Deacon, because we all know KeKe got a big ass mouth!"

"What, Big Lee?" KeKe whined. "I ain't said, nothing!"

Big Lee looked over at KeKe then rolled her eyes.

"Come on outside with me to smoke a cigarette," Big Lee demanded. "I'm gon' cuss you out in private."

Deacon grabbed his cigarettes and drink then followed behind his sister. He looked back at KeKe and glared at her 'cause he knew she had ran her mouth. It was her fault that he was going to get the cussin' of his life, but he needed to learn how to shut the fuck up!

"Bitch, you talk to damn much!" Deacon cussed. "You need to do what you know how to do best with your mouth, and that's keep a dick in that muthafucka because you run them dick beaters too fucking much!"

"Fuck you, Deacon!" KeKe snapped. "It ain't my fault that when you get a taste of this pussy, you want to confess all your sins and tell everyone's business. I didn't tell Big Lee that you said—"

"Bitch, shut up!" Deacon boomed. "You was about to tell some shit that would probably get me further cussed out! I need to get me a new prostitute 'cause you tell every fucking thing that you know!"

"I ain't told your wife that you're taking care of me, have I?" KeKe seethed as she crossed her arms in front of her.

"You better not tell her, or she's going to kick your ass!" Deacon replied smugly. "Now I don't ask for too much from you. I just ask that you suck my dick because these young hoes like to reach in your pocket while they're doing it and try to steal all of your money."

"Take all of your money?" Big Lee repeated and laughed.

"Yeah, all your money! They don't know how to just take a few dollars to make a nigga think he lost some shit," Deacon explained. "They take the whole wad and may cuff your wallet too. Get your credit card statement at the end of the month and this bitch done charged up your shit, getting a True Religion outfit and some Ugg boots."

"You dumb as hell, Deacon." Big Lee continued to laugh. "You know you make me sick!"

"I'm sorry, but I'm just telling the fucking truth! This bitch wants to play 'that's my best friend' and tell you some shit. Did that bitch tell you how she sucked my dick while I was on the toilet taking a shit!" Deacon shouted. KeKe looked down the bar at Deacon because she had been walked away from the conversation. She knew that Deacon told her those things in confidence, but KeKe didn't know how to keep her mouth closed.

"I don't know why you told that bitch shit!" Big Lee fussed. "You know I had to beat her ass before about telling my business. You're a married man and can't afford to have Jazzy find out about y'all."

"Jazzy ain't gon' do shit but make me sleep on the couch for about a week," Deacon replied confidently. "I'll pack an overnight bag and say that I'm going to a hotel. That bitch will turn into the exorcist and levitate around the room."

"I'm done talking to you because you got my side hurting," Big Lee called out, laughing. She could always count on her big brother to make her laugh, and this time was no different.

CHAPTER SIX

ManMan and his crew walked into the lounge, ready to party on a Friday night. Lay looked up and noticed one of her earrings in ManMan's ear and damn near lost it. It wasn't like he didn't have a pair of diamond earrings of his own, but Lay's studs were the size of dimes, and they were three karats. Her mama had a keen sense of things, and Lay was afraid if her mama saw that earring in ManMan's ear, she would ask Lay about hers. Then Lay would have to explain that she didn't have her earrings in her possession.

ManMan looked over and noticed Lay behind the bar looking good as usual. She had on a hunter-green wrap dress that clung to her breasts and curves just right. The v-cut at the top was giving sexy cleavage along with the earth-tone colored necklace that draped down her DD cups, and the site made ManMan's mouth water. He was a few years older than Lay and graduated from high school two years before her. He used to try to push up on her, but there was a bit of bad blood between their mothers, so Lay knew he was off limits. Big Lee had taken Cecil from Jane, ManMan's mother, back in the day, and when Big Lee had gotten pregnant, Jane and her girls tried to jump on Big Lee. However, they didn't know Lee Ann Wilson had a crazy ass mama, and they learned that day when she pulled up with a 357 Magnum in her hand.

ManMan walked up to the bar and smiled at Lay. He was about six feet three with sugar-cookie colored skin. His light-brown, curly hair and green eyes had all of the girls in the hood chasing after him—except Lay. Like her mama, Lay didn't like light-skinned niggas, because Big Lee always said they were sneaky and conniving and not to be trusted. She felt that way because she had her heart broken by a light-skinned boy when she was a freshman in high school, so after that situation, she vowed to never mess with another light-skinned man as long as she lived.

"I know this muthafucka didn't," Lay mumbled, watching ManMan speak to a few people.

"What you talking about, Lay?" asked Big Lee because she noticed how hard her daughter was clocking ManMan.

"Nothing, Mama," Lay replied, placing drinks on a tray. "I just noticed that pink boy had walked through the door." Big Lee studied her daughter because the look on Lay's face told a different story. She knew her daughter, and the mean grimace she was giving said something totally different.

"Hey, Lay," said ManMan, moving down the bar. Lay looked up at him, focusing her eyes on her earring.

"What's up? What can I get for you?" Lay asked dryly.

"It ain't about what you can get for me," ManMan said sleazily. "It's about what I can do for you."

Big Lee raised an eyebrow because she was interested in knowing what he meant by that statement.

“I ain’t buying shit you selling.” Lay scoffed. “And I know you fixed that dice game, so what you want to order? I got other customers waiting.”

“Damn, Lay! You think that less of me?” asked ManMan, smiling.

“Look, either order, or get out my face!” Lay snapped, turning her lips up at him. “I don’t have time to play with you. Especially, since you’re trying to throw some shit up in my face! You better be lucky my mama don’t know what’s going on, ‘cause if she did” —Lay looked over at Big Lee who was talking to one of the customers—”she would have been come around that corner and got my shit back!” Lay crossed her arms in front of her defensively with a mean mug on her face.

“What’s up, princess?” Whisper asked, walking up on ManMan. He mugged ManMan up and down and stood beside him. Whisper didn’t like ManMan, because his brother Boogie got him locked up. He helped Boogie get on a lick, and when he got caught, Boogie rolled over on Whisper.

“Hi, Godfather,” Lay replied and smirked. She noticed how uncomfortable ManMan looked, and she loved every minute of it.

“Is that your situation?” asked Whisper, pointing to the earring in ManMan’s ear.

“Yeap,” Lay replied, turning up her lips.

“What the fuck you doing with her shit in your ear?” Whisper snapped. “That ain’t the way the game goes, but yo’ peoples’ some bitch ass niggas, so it can be expected.”

“Aye, Whisper, I ain’t got no beef with you,” ManMan replied, throwing up his hands in front of him. “I just came over to order a few drinks and tell Lay how beautiful she looked in that dress."

Whisper lifted an eyebrow. "Well I got a problem with yo' bitch ass. Why you got my baby's earring in your ear? Ew Baby's stupid ass pawned them muthafuckas to you, so that means they're supposed to be put up somewhere safe. Not sitting in your big ass ear!" Whisper seethed.

"Ah, it's safe," ManMan replied. "Ain't no nigga stupid enough to run up on me!"

Whisper looked at him in disbelief and laughed.

"I see about six niggas in here that would run up on your ass with no hesitation," Lay spat annoyed. "You got this hood fucked up! But keep playing, and you'll find out!"

ManMan looked back at Whisper, who was still posted up in a defensive stance. Then he looked over at Lay, who he wanted now more than ever. "Can I get two buckets of beer, one Bud Light and the other Budweiser. Also, I want a set-up of Patron, the biggest bottle you have, and lime juice as my chaser," ManMan uttered off. Lay turned to go get his order ready. "I ain't got no beef with you, Whisper, straight up, for real! Why you sweating me, OG?" ManMan asked defensively.

"'Cause my baby told me how you one-two'd Ew Baby, and you know that's a violation, don't you?" Whisper retorted. ManMan turned to face Whisper because he wanted to look him straight in the eye when he pleaded his case. He stood about three inches taller than Whisper, but he knew Whisper would knock his ass out.

"I did nothing of the sort. Ew Baby crapped out and lost her money. That's it; that's all," ManMan explained. "It's unfortunate that

Lay let Ew Baby get her in a jam, but I'm a businessman, and I have to protect my investment. I would lose so much money if I felt sorry for all those poor muthafuckas who lost their money at my house. But Ew Baby and Lay are grown women, and they know what it do when they walk through the door." Whisper looked at ManMan and wanted to slap the smug look off of his face, but what ManMan said was correct, because he didn't know if James fixed the game or not.

"You made a valid point," Whisper replied. "But that don't give you the right to walk around with my baby's shit in your ear. So the next time I see you, it better not be in there. Flat out!"

"I got you, Whisper," ManMan replied as Lay sat his order on the counter.

"That'll be sixty-five dollars," said Lay. ManMan reached into his pocket and pulled out a wad of money. He peeled off a couple of hundred-dollar bills and handed them to her.

"Keep the change," said ManMan arrogantly and smiled.

Lay took the money and looked at him, unamused. "I would have been more impressed if you'd given me that earring in your ear," said Lay smugly as she rolled her eyes and walked away. Whisper laughed as he watched ManMan's smile fade to a frown.

"She don't impress easily. We been getting bread." Whisper scoffed before he walked off. Lay was putting her tip in the jar when her phone made a tinkling sound.

Text Message: *I see that nigga ManMan grinning all up in your face. Lay smiled as she looked around the bar.*

Text Message: *Lay: He ain't making no noise, but what's up with you?*

Lay pressed send then went back to work. She waited on a couple of customers when the tinkling sound from her phone went off again. A smile instantly came across her face because he responded back quickly. She grabbed a Bud Light out of the cooler and picked up her phone. She walked up to the bar and gave it to Deacon, who was watching some slim chick that just came through the door.

"Ewww… weee… niece!" yelled Deacon with a big smile on his face. "That slim goody right there gon' make me spend all my pocket money tonight." Lay looked over at the woman who was wearing a red tube dress and a full-length fur coat. She didn't have much body to her, but that's the way Deacon liked them. His wife, Jazzy, was slim when they first got together, but after she had the kids, her butt and hips spread, and her breasts remained small.

"Auntie gon' kick your ass, Unc," Lay replied, laughing as she checked her message.

Text Message: *I can't tell the way he's over here talking all shit about you. He said you be clocking him and was all up on his tip the other day.*

Lay looked over to where ManMan and his crew were chilling. His best friend, Byrd, was standing next to him and looked up at Lay and smiled. She turned up her lips and threw her head back at him then sent him a response back.

Text Message: *Lay: Now you know he ain't told you no shit like that! That nigga be checking for me, but he gets no play! So what's up? Are we on for tonight?*

Lay sent the message and put her phone down. She began to wash the dirty glasses that were sitting in the sink when Big Lee came and sat down on her stool.

"Baby girl, can you get your mama a cold drink of water? Those niggas over there taking shots of 1800, and they made my ass take two," she explained, pulling out a cigarette. She fired it up, taking a long drag from it.

"Mama! You know if those people come in here, we gon' get fined for you smoking inside the lounge," Lay fussed, putting a glass of water in front of her mother.

Big Lee raised an eyebrow at her daughter. "I don't give a fuck about a fine. I'll pay the muthafucka then tell the people to kiss my ass at the same time!" Big Lee replied before taking a drink of water.

Lay's phone went off, and she instantly looked down at it.

"Daaaamn! You sure did move quick to see that message!"

Lay looked up at her mother and smiled.

Text Message: *You better keep it that way, too! I don't want to have to fuck you up for giving my goodies away. Same time?*

Lay smiled as she read the message. She looked up at Byrd as she bit her bottom lip. *This nigga straight sprung,* thought Lay as she stood motionlessly, smiling at her phone. She quickly texted back because she wished it was quitting time already.

Text Message: *Lay: Yeah. And you better bring some gas too.*

"That nigga must be talking that good shit," Big Lee crooned, hitting her cigarette and laughing.

"What nigga?" Whisper asked, taking the cigarette out of Big

Lee's hand.

"How you know it's a nigga?" Lay asked with a smirk on her face. Whisper hit the cigarette then looked over at Big Lee.

"Look at her face. She's absolutely smitten," Big Lee pointed out. "The only time a woman smiles at her phone like that is when a nigga is texting her some good shit!"

"What nigga texting my niece some good shit?" Deacon asked loudly, walking up to them.

"Some nigga that's texting Lay," Whisper replied.

"You know what? Y'all needs to mind y'all own business; no disrespect, Mama," said Lay, holding her hand out in front of her mother.

Big Lee smiled as her baby's face beamed with happiness.

"He better have some money!" Deacon demanded. "'Cause don't nobody got time for no broke ass niggas! Yo' mama specialized in that shit and got it on lock!"

Big Lee hit Deacon on the arm while Whisper fell out laughing.

"I don't know what you laughing for, Whisper. He's probably talking about you," Big Lee replied smugly. Whisper frowned up at Big Lee because it was obvious she was mad.

"You know that nigga ain't talking about me, so you can gone somewhere with that hip shit," Whisper spat and smirked.

Big Lee looked at Whisper with a disapproving look on her face, but when she looked into his pretty brown eyes, a smile tried to dance across her lips.

"You know your tough ass want to smile at me. Why don't you go on and smile for daddy?"

Big Lee tried her best not to smile, but she just couldn't help herself. Her lips spread across her face, and a big smile finally graced their presence. She didn't like showing Whisper that he could pull her strings. However, she liked every minute of it, and that's why she was so in love with him.

CHAPTER SEVEN

"Come on so I can get you home," said Whisper, putting his hand on the small of Big Lee's back. She was drunk and halfway in control, but Whisper knew she was done.

"You gon' tuck me in?" asked Big Lee, grabbing his crotch. Whisper looked down at her then kissed her on the lips.

"Don't I always tuck you in, baby?" he replied as they gazed into each other's eyes. Every time Big Lee looked at Whisper, she could see Lay in his face. If only he had spoken up, she would have told Whisper the truth and married him instead of Cecil.

"Make sure our baby has someone escorting her home. I know she lives around the corner, but a nigga will try anything once," Big Lee uttered.

"Aye, Lay! Who you leaving with?" asked Whisper, staring at her.

"I'm gone leave with Ew Baby," she replied.

"But Ew Baby left about an hour ago. So how you leaving with her?" Whisper questioned. The buzzer went off, and Whisper checked the surveillance cameras. He noticed Byrd standing in front of the door, and a smirk came over his face. "Alright, Lay, I see you!" Whisper walked over to the door and glanced back at his goddaughter.

"What, Whisper?" she asked, smiling as he opened the door. Byrd looked up with a big smile on his face.

"Hey, you—" he said, looking up at Whisper. The look on Byrd's face instantly went to shock as Whisper stared at him with a smirk on his face.

"What you want, lil' nigga?" asked Whisper, mugging Byrd up and down.

"Hey, Whisper. I-I-I… just came to get Layloni," Byrd stuttered.

"For what? It's almost two o'clock in the morning," Whisper spat sternly. "The only thing on a lil' nigga's mind this time of night is getting up in some guts or getting up in some guts." Whisper folded his arms in front of him as Byrd stood with a nervous look on his face.

"Leave that boy alone, Whisper," Big Lee called out then laughed. She pushed Whisper out of the way and stared Byrd up and down. "Come on in, baby."

Byrd slid past Whisper and Big Lee then he looked back at both of them. "We about to go, Lay," Big Lee said, watching her daughter. She already knew they were creeping around when she caught Byrd leaving Lay's apartment. Big Lee made sure that if nothing else, her girls weren't going to get played because she was always brutally honest with them about men. She didn't want her girls to make the same mistakes she did as a young woman, and she made damn sure they didn't get pregnant. "Uhhh, Byrd," Big Lee called out, smugly.

"Ma'am?" he replied.

"Make sure you strap up before you stick yo' dick in my daughter," Big Lee advised. Whisper looked at Byrd and smiled, showing all of his gold teeth.

"Mama!" Lay screamed, feeling completely embarrassed. "You are so embarrassing!"

"What's embarrassing is having to go to the clinic and get a shot in your ass 'cause that nigga burned you!" Big Lee replied before Whisper pulled her out the door.

"Y'all be good!" Whisper added, pointing at Byrd. Lay quickly walked over to the door and locked it. She felt like both her mother and godfather did too much, but there was nothing she could do about it. She didn't want them to further embarrass her anymore, so she made sure they couldn't come back inside by putting the chain on the door. Lay turned and leaned her back up against it, studying Byrd's face for a second.

"You was scared as hell, wasn't you?" Lay teased, smiling.

"I wasn't scared, but uh…" Byrd licked his lips.

"Nigga, please! Whisper had you shook up," she joked.

"Whisper ain't have me shit!" Byrd scoffed, walking up on Lay. He grabbed her by the waist and pulled her into him. "Now your mama… That's a different story. Everybody knows not to fuck with Big Lee!"

"The only reason people are scared of my mama is because of her brothers," Lay replied and laughed.

"Naw, Lay. I've seen your mama knock a nigga out for trying to skip out on a tab," he insisted. Lay studied his face as he pulled her in closer. He towered over her with his six-foot-four-inch frame. Lay loved his dark-chocolate skin and the nicely trimmed goatee he sported, but his long braids that reached his shoulders were the end all to be all to her.

Byrd bent down, kissing Lay on the lips. He slid his hands down her back until they landed on her butt, then he gripped it. Lay wrapped her arms around his neck, inviting his tongue in her mouth. She went up on her tiptoes because she wanted to feel more involved. Lay had this thing about climbing up men with long, lanky bodies, and Byrd loved the way she climbed. He swept her up in his arms, moving through the bar with ease. He knew they had a time limit to get to the apartment next door because Teke would be coming to clean up soon.

"Wait a minute. I have to grab my purse," Lay remembered.

"Can't we get it later? You know Teke gon' be here in a minute," Byrd replied. "I don't want him to know we jamming, 'cause whenever he comes around the corner, he gon' expect me to throw him something. Whisper told me don't give him shit, but you know Teke."

Lay laughed as he put her down. "Y'all better leave Teke alone. My mama makes sure he has all the dope he needs. She passes it out to his ass like they do meds at a nursing home," Lay joked then laughed.

Byrd smiled as he watched Lay go over to the bar. "You looking nice in that dress, Ms. Wilson." Byrd moaned, rubbing his hands together. It moved effortlessly with every twist of her hips as she did her best walk across the floor. She accompanied the dress with a pair of burgundy suede knee boots with a wooden wedged heel to show her grown-woman swag.

"Why thank you, Brian Byrd," she replied, walking toward him.

"You and my mama are the only people I like hearing say my

name," Byrd admitted and smiled. He put his arm around Lay's shoulders and gripped her breast. She lifted an eyebrow at him because he'd never done anything like this before.

"You're really going to like the way I call your name in a few minutes," Lay bragged smugly with a smirk on her face. They grabbed each other's hand like it was a natural motion then walked over to the apartment next door to the bar.

Lay pushed Byrd down on the bed and smiled at him seductively. He quickly took his gold Cuban links off his neck, placing them on the nightstand. Next, he grabbed the bottom of this shirt and pulled it over his head. His dick was already hard, but he knew Lay was going to want to mess around a little before she gave him the nookie.

"Where them joints at?" Lay asked, untying her dress. She opened it up, exposing a black lace bra and panty set, and it made Byrd's manhood throb. Her beautiful skin shimmered from the sporadic light that shined through the window.

"Yeah, I got 'em," Byrd replied, pulling a couple of gold boys out his pocket. Lay smiled as she dropped her dress to the floor then rubbed up and down her body. She gripped her breasts and looked at Byrd suggestively.

"I want to do something a little different tonight," said Lay, unfastening her bra. She let her DD's fall free from the cups as she watched a big grin spread across Byrd's face.

"I'm with whatever you want, lil' big mama," Byrd replied. "Just come over here, and let me put one of those pretty muthafuckas in my mouth!"

Lay laughed as she threw her bra on the floor. She grabbed her nipples, pinching them enticingly at him. "How bad you want this?" she asked, teasingly.

"Girl!" Byrd sang, sitting up. "You better quit playing with me and come here!" He reached out and grabbed her arm, pulling Lay to him. He smiled at her because he liked how she teased him. The way she played tough was so cute to him, but when she got in his arms, she melted like butter. He knew Lay wasn't checking for anyone else, because she was always sweating him. He had a few chicks whose thoughts he entertained, but they were of no interest to him.

Lay was about to graduate from college, and he was about to graduate from Ranken with a Bachelor of Science in Applied Management for carpentry and building construction technology. They would be the power couple of the hood if they made it official, but he wasn't ready to settle down, because his pockets weren't quite right. He already hustled up on a half a million dollars, but if he were going to be with Layloni, that wasn't enough in his opinion. Big Lee was a multi-millionaire, so Lay was used to having the finest things in life. She already drove a BMW 3 Series, and she was driving those when she was fifteen years old. All he needed was another half to be comfortable with claiming his queen because he wasn't trying to play the boyfriend/girlfriend game. He truly loved Lay and wanted to ask her to marry him when the time was right.

Lay stood in front of Byrd and leaned down to kiss him. He fell back and pulled her down on top of him, falling into the pillows. The gaze they held was intense because they both had one thing on their minds. It was about to go down and would last until the wee hours of the night.

CHAPTER EIGHT

"Well, good morning," said Big Lee, walking into the kitchen. She smiled hard because Whisper was standing at the stove in his boxers and tank top, cooking her breakfast.

"Good morning, baby," Whisper replied, leaning down to kiss her lips. "I was trying to surprise you with breakfast in bed."

"Ah, baby, you're so sweet." She smiled, kissing him again. "If I didn't know any better, I would—"

"What you didn't know?" Whisper questioned, lifting his eyebrow.

Big Lee smiled as she walked away because she was about to say something smart mouthed. "When I woke up, I thought you'd ducked out on me again," Big Lee replied, pouring herself a glass of grape juice.

"Don't start, Ann. No, I didn't leave you. I'm in the kitchen, cooking your ass something to eat." Whisper scoffed.

"And you look good doing it. There's nothing like a man cooking breakfast in boxers, a tank top, socks, and house shoes! That's my type of nigga, and that's some sexy shit!" Big Lee called out and laughed.

"You got that shit right, and when you divorce that bitch ass nigga, I'll be able to put a ring on your finger and really show you what type of nigga I am."

Big Lee was taken aback by the comment. Whisper had never said anything like that to her before, so it kind of threw her off. It wasn't that she didn't like what he had said to her, but it was the way he came out of nowhere with his confession.

"Did I fuck you too good last night or something, Whisper? Where is all of this coming from?" asked Big Lee, confused. Whisper turned to face her with two plates of food in his hand. He'd made scrambled eggs with cheese, turkey sausage patties, fried potatoes with onions, green peppers and cheese, and pancakes.

Big Lee stared at all the food on their plates as he put one down in front of her. "Well damn, Whisper, baby! I guess you're serious about what you're saying because a breakfast like this lets a bitch know you're serious. I put it down last night!" Big Lee jumped up out of her chair and started twerking.

Whisper laughed because he liked how she could be silly sometimes. Here and now lately, something had been bothering her, and when he asked what was wrong, she would play it off as nothing. He loved her with all of his heart because she held him down while he was in jail. Ralph and Rico made sure he didn't want for nothing, and Big Lee was right there with them. If only he would have told her not to marry Cecil.

"Come sit down and eat your food before it gets cold," Whisper ordered, laughing. "We still have to get our morning session in after breakfast." Big Lee smiled as she walked over to the table, and as she sat down, she noticed Lay cutting across the parking lot toward her apartment.

Where is that little heffa coming from? Big Lee wondered. She walked over to the window to investigate further. She looked toward the alley and noticed Byrd headed toward his car. "That little freak! She spent the night in the apartment."

Whisper got up and walked over to the window, looking out over Big Lee's shoulder. "That little nigga!" Whisper shouted and laughed. Big Lee looked up at him with a frown on her face.

"That little nigga is right!" Big Lee scoffed. "He's been sniffing at my baby's skirt ever since he could walk."

"He sounds like me with you," Whisper replied, laughing. Then he kissed the top of Big Lee's head before pulling her over to the table. "Sit down and finish your breakfast, woman, and you're going to tell me what's been going on with you. I've noticed how moody you've been lately, and I know you're not tripping off of Amber."

Big Lee sat down and poked at her food then put her fork down. She grabbed her cigarettes off the table and fired one up.

"You know I don't like to talk to you about Cecil," said Big Lee, taking a hit of her cigarette.

"I know, Ann, but when it's affecting you like this, it becomes a concern for me," Whisper explained. He took her cigarette and hit it as he stared at her intently. She looked over at him and smiled because he always did that to her. She took out another cigarette and fired it up because she knew he wasn't going to give it back.

"Cecil's been worrying me to talk to my brothers about letting his little brother get a piece of the action for a cheaper price. He's on his way home, and he's trying to solidify himself a block or two with

Geechie," Lay explained.

"Why don't he talk to your brothers himself? He knows Deacon and Craig personally," Whisper replied. "Cecil was fucking with them before he even stepped to you. Besides, Craig hates when Cecil does that shit, and I don't know why you married his bitch ass in the first place!"

"Because your bitch ass didn't stop me!" Big Lee blurted out.

Whisper looked over at her, shocked. "Seriously, Ann? You and your brothers have been saying that for years, but you had a child with that man, and it appeared that you guys were happy," Whisper explained.

"How the hell was I happy when I was still fucking with you?" Big Lee asked frankly. "Now you know one thing about me; I'm loyal to a fault. I didn't want to leave Cecil in jail hanging, and if I would have known Ew Baby was his daughter before I said I do, let's just say the marriage wouldn't have taken place." Big Lee hit her cigarette, feeling more frustrated.

What everyone didn't know was that Big Lee went and had her marriage annulled a week after she found out about his other child. He lied to her about the situation when she'd found out Patricia was pregnant. She didn't know her at the time, but word had gotten back to her that Cecil had another girl pregnant, and when he moved her into the neighborhood, Big Lee knew something wasn't right.

Craig immediately took her to the courthouse when she told him that Ew Baby was Cecil's daughter. Craig never liked Big Lee being with Cecil, but he had no say so in the matter. Everything happened so fast, and Big Lee just couldn't take the pressure. She married Cecil, then Ew Baby was taken into custody right after that. It was too much for Big Lee to bear, so her big brother stepped in and took matters into his own hands.

"You tell that nigga that he needs to talk to Craig directly. Deacon just gon' put his ass off, saying he'll talk to everyone else," Whisper replied and laughed.

"I'm gon' go talk to Craig and Deacon because shit ain't gon' be the same when he comes home. You know me and that nigga ain't together for real. He got a whole bitch over on the southside, so he needs to set up shop over there," said Big Lee, putting out her cigarette. Her breast was partially exposed out of her tank top, and Whisper took notice.

Whisper put out his cigarette and grabbed Big Lee by the hand. He pulled her over to him and kissed her on the lips. He continued to kiss down her face, concentrating on her neck. His kisses lingered as he traveled down to her breasts, his favorite thing to play with. He pulled one of them out of the side of her tank top and placed her nipple in his mouth. She moaned as he flickered his tongue against her nub, sending stimulation all through her body. Big Lee rubbed the back of his head because she enjoyed being pleasured. Whisper looked up and kissed her on the lips then moved over to her other nipple, sucking it relentlessly.

"Ewww, that feels so good." Big Lee moaned, massaging Whisper's shoulders.

He stood up and grabbed her by the hand because he was ready for round two. He turned her around and bent her over the table. Next, he pulled up her tank top and pulled down his boxers, ready to help her relieve some stress. Whisper rubbed his hard on against the folds of her wetness then slid himself inside of her with ease. He marveled at how good she felt, and wanted to stay there for the rest of his life. Whisper had started to realize that he fucked up, and he needed to get on track in order to make things right between him and Big Lee. She was his woman whether everyone knew it or not. Cecil would definitely be an issue that he'd have to deal with in a matter of time. However, Whisper wasn't worried about it, because Big Lee had made it perfectly clear that he was the one she wanted.

"Oh, you feel so good." Whisper moaned, leaning down to kiss the middle of her back. "You're so wet!"

"I know, right! That's because you know how to please her." Big Lee groaned.

Whisper pulled back slowly then eased himself back inside of her. He liked to go slow and tease her because he liked to hear her beg for the dick.

"Here you go, playing these reindeer games," Big Lee complained. "Quit playing with me and give it to me, daddy!"

Whisper smiled as he listened to her moan because he kept easing himself in and out of her slowly. He grabbed her hips and sped up his pace as his thighs made a smacking sound against hers. He knew she was happy with his pace because all he heard from her were moan and groans.

"Yassss, Jamal!" she called out passionately as his rod hit a quick right into her curve. He was the only one who had that type of depth action, and it drove Big Lee crazy every time he did it. It was a wonder she hadn't had more kids by him the way he dicked her down so good.

"Whose pussy is this, Lee Ann?" Whisper called out as he smacked her on the ass with his hand. She looked back at him and laughed because he already knew the answer to the question.

"Don't play with me, nigga! You know this is your pussy," she replied, pushing back against him.

He knew that it was getting good to her because that's when she became a willing participant. They went at it hot and heavy as sweat poured down their bodies. They were so into each other that they didn't even hear the front door open and close.

"Ah, damn, Mama!" Lay shouted.

"Ah, day'um, Whisper!" Ew Baby cooed as everyone froze.

"Get the fuck up out my house!" Big Lee yelled. "And don't come back until I call you!"

Both girls laughed as they ran downstairs where their rooms were located. Even though they shared an apartment around the corner, they still came over to hang out in their old rooms from time to time. Big Lee stayed at her house in the hood the most because she liked being close to her family, and that's where most of her money was made.

"Should we stop?" asked Whisper, looking down at Big Lee.

"Hell naw!" she replied, still working him in and out of her wet walls. "Those little bitches know better than to come over in the mornings unannounced. I told them to always call first."

Whisper laughed as he quickened the pace because he was about to nut before they were so rudely interrupted. They went at it a few more minutes until Big Lee made a certain sound. Whisper knew she was about to orgasm, and he was right there too.

"Oh, Jamal..." She moaned as her body began to tingle. Her orgasm crept from the center of her core then spread throughout her body. "Oh yeah, baby... Uhhh..."

"Ah, damn, Ann... Oh yeah..." Whisper moaned.

The girls laughed as they heard their mother and Whisper finish having sex. It reminded them of when they were teenagers, and he would sneak over in the middle of the night.

Before their mother bought the big house in the Central West End, she had bought up all the houses on their block and strategically placed everyone so that all her family would be close. The way the houses were set up, everyone's back yard was connected. Big Lee had the houses next to their old house torn down and a new house built over two housing plots. Rico lived in the house next door to Big Lee, Whisper lived in the one next to him, and Ralph lived in the last house on the alley. Deacon and his family lived in the house they grew up in across Aldine Avenue on the corner of Billups Avenue, and Craig lived in the house next to him. Deacon and Craig's backyard were connected, along with a plot of land next to Craig's house. Cam and Ax lived in a four-family flat that was converted into two townhouse apartments on the corner, across from Big Lee, and Lay and Ew Baby shared a three-bedroom converted apartment next door to their uncles.

Their family had the whole block on lock with other family and friends (allies) surrounding them throughout the Ville. A parking lot for their cars sat across the street from Deacon and Craig's house, where everyone could park their cars. Big Lee converted a huge vacant lot into a park with playground equipment and benches for the neighborhood children. The lot across from it was converted into a full basketball court because they needed to stay close to home, and her brothers loved to play the game. She wanted to make their lives convenient and safe, and when you pretty much owned everything in a ten-block radius, you definitely could control everything that went on around it.

CHAPTER NINE

Ew Baby pulled up in front of the pump at the gas station on MLK and Cora. She had a green BMW 3 Series, something like Lay's. Big Lee tried not to make too much of a difference between the girls, but of course, there were certain things that Lay got that Ew Baby didn't get. She noticed Byrd and ManMan sitting in Byrd's blue Challenger. They had the windows down, so you could see inside of the car. Byrd had the presidential tents on all of his windows because he didn't like people being able to see in his car. Ew Baby saw Byrd's car parked outside the lounge last night, and Lay didn't come home until this morning.

Ew Baby got out of her car and walked around to the pump. She noticed ManMan looking at her, so she poked her titties out and stood up straight. She wasn't blessed with big girls, but she had enough for a handful. Her long, slender build, with just enough hips and butt, made men definitely take notice. She had light-brown graham cracker colored skin that was smooth and flawless, and her big eyes and full lips were the finishing touches to her beautiful face.

Ew Baby swung her new long, thirty-six-inch Brazilian sew-in over her shoulder, then she reached over and grabbed the pump, inserting it into her gas tank. She leaned over, exposing her tramp stamp of flowers from up under her coat. She looked back to see if ManMan or Byrd were paying her any attention, but they were too involved with their conversation to notice.

"I don't know why Lay won't give me no play." ManMan frowned, looking over at Ew Baby. "I have everything a woman could want. I'm fine as a muthafucka, I got good hair, and I'm light skinned."

"That's the problem. Lay don't like light-skinned niggas," Byrd replied smugly. "She never did. I remember when we were little, she wouldn't play with the light-skinned kids for a long time when we were in elementary school."

ManMan looked at him funny. "Since when have you become an expert on Lay?" asked ManMan with his brow furrowed.

"I grew up with her, remember? My mama works at Big Lee's daycare," Byrd reminded him, looking over at Ew Baby. "Uuunnn… Pull up your pants!" shouted Byrd out of the window. Ew Baby swung around, placing her hand on her hip.

"Who you talking too?" asked Ew Baby with an attitude. "'Cause I know you're not talking to me!" She smiled as ManMan leaned up to look at her. "What you looking at, ManMan?" Ew Baby smiled.

"I was trying to see if Lay was with you," he replied, leaning back down in the seat. Ew Baby cut her eyes at him before she rolled them hard. Lay wasn't checking for ManMan, 'cause she wasn't interested in him, but for some strange reason, he couldn't accept it. Besides, Lay was Byrd's chick, and once they decided to make it known to everyone, there would definitely be some tension between ManMan and Byrd.

Byrd got out of the car and walked over to Ew Baby. She crossed her arms in front of her body because she knew he wanted to question her about Lay. She thought they made a cute couple, and she couldn't understand why they were keeping things a secret. If Byrd were her man, she'd proudly make it known. Hoes were always in his face, and Ew Baby thought it very disrespectful.

"What's up, Ew Baby? Where's Lay?" Byrd asked, walking up on her.

"She rode up to Bonne Terre to see her daddy," Ew Baby replied.

"Ah yeah, who did she go with?"

"She went with Mama to run defense." Ew Baby laughed. "Mama hates for Lay to go on those visits, but when she don't want to be bothered with Cecil, she'll make Lay go with her." Ew Baby looked past Byrd to see if ManMan were paying attention to them. "Say, I noticed your car was parked behind the lounge this morning when I came home. What's up with that?"

Byrd smiled at Ew Baby because it was apparent she was fishing for something. "I jumped in the car with ManMan last night. I knew a nigga wasn't gon' fuck with it if I left it there," Byrd explained.

"Hmph… I guess I believe you," Ew Baby replied, hanging up her pump.

"Can you do me a favor?" asked Byrd, walking closer to her.

"Why you walking all up on me?" asked Ew Baby, frowning. Byrd pushed her in the arm as they both laughed.

"Quit playing, lil' girl, and give this to Lay for me," said Byrd, handing her a small brown paper bag.

"What's this?" Ew Baby asked, looking at him skeptically.

"None of your business," he replied. "Just give it to her."

"A'ight, but next time, I'm gon' charge you a fee!" Ew Baby scoffed and smirked. Byrd laughed as he walked back over to his car. *Lay must have fucked that nigga real good last night if he sending her packages,* thought Ew Baby. She hung up her pump and got into her car. She was going to wait until she got in the house before she looked in Lay's goodie bag because she didn't want Byrd to see her being nosy.

****

Lay was sitting at the table, looking at all the people in the visiting room. There were all types sitting at tables, either anxiously waiting or visiting with their loved ones. Big Lee had already told Lay that they wouldn't be at the visit long. She just wanted her daughter to come so that Cecil wouldn't make a big scene.

What the fuck is Lay doing here? thought Cecil as he walked toward them. *This bitch must be up to something if she brought this girl with her.* "Well if it isn't my two favorite girls," said Cecil, smiling as he walked up to the table. Both women looked at him with the same smirk on their faces. "Daaamn, a nigga can't get a hug or something?"

Lay laughed as she stood up to hug her father. It had been a while since she'd made the drive to see him, so she felt like she should at least give him a hug. "Hi, Daddy," said Lay, wrapping her arms around his waist. Cecil hugged her back, and he planted a kiss on her forehead. Cecil turned to face Big Lee.

"You know we don't get down like that, Cecil, so we ain't even about to play pretend," said Big Lee, turning up her lips at him.

"I was hoping you would have had a change of heart when you saw me," replied Cecil, walking over to her with a smile on his face. He leaned down and kissed her forehead then placed his hand on the back of her neck and squeezed hard.

"Get off me, nigga," Big Lee snapped, pushing his hand aside. "You got twenty minutes to say what you need to say, then we out of here." Big Lee looked down at her gold and diamond Rolex watch, checking the time. Cecil laughed as he sat down at the table because Big Lee was being extra as usual.

"Your mama sure hasn't changed," Cecil announced. "She's always about business."

"So if you know that, you'll get to talking," Big Lee replied dryly.

Lay jumped up from her seat because she wasn't about to get in the middle of their stuff. "I'm about to go get something out of the vending machine," Lay blurted out. She quickly jumped up from the table and walked off before either of them could stop her. They both watched as Lay went to the back of the room where the vending machines were located. The tension between them was obvious, and Big Lee just really didn't want to be there.

"Can you just forgive me, Lee Ann? I'm tired of it always being a battle when we talk," Cecil fussed.

"If your daughter can forgive you, then I'll consider it," Big Lee replied.

"Does she know?" Cecil asked defensively. Big Lee looked at him with a frown on her face.

"Fuck naw, Lay don't know," Big Lee replied smugly. "Just like she don't know you ain't her daddy." Cecil's jaw tightened as he glared at Big Lee. He wanted to grab her around the neck and squeeze tightly in order to get his point across. However, the best course of action would be to just smooth things over for right now.

"So you keeping secrets from Lay? Secrets that could completely fuck up the situation you got at home," said Cecil smugly. "'Cause the way I see it, if Lay don't know Whisper's her father, nine times out of ten, Whisper don't know either. It would be tragic for them to find out the truth right before his death."

Big Lee looked at him, shocked. "Are you really saying this to me right now?" asked Big Lee, annoyed. "Because we both know that Whisper ain't scared of your ass. Me begging him not to kill you is the reason you're sitting here right now!"

"It wasn't his place to step into business between a grown man and his woman. So what if I smacked the shit out of you?" Cecil frowned. "You were mouthing off to me—"

"See, that's why you gon' always lose when it comes to me. 'Cause you never have the right to put your hands on me! And with that frame of mind you got, that's why we'll never be together. So how about you save all that hip shit for your bitch over on the southside. 'Cause I ain't trying to hear shit you got to say! Especially if it ain't making me no money," Big Lee retorted. She got up from her seat and straightened her shirt.

"I just want you to ask your brothers to show some love to me." Cecil sighed, looking defeated. "I'm just trying to situate myself before I come home."

"I'm holding you down while you're in jail. Isn't that enough?" asked Big Lee plainly.

He looked up at her smugly. "Nope! Check it. This is how we're going to play it. I'm gon' send Geechie to see you, and I'm hoping that you'll show some love and help me get a few houses together. You know I don't have a lot of money, Lee Ann," Cecil huffed.

"I know… Because I pulled my titty out of your mouth," she replied smugly. "Aye, Lay, we out of here!"

"Can we wait until I eat my snacks?" Lay whined, holding her stuff up in the air.

"I'm gon' be in the car waiting, so eat that shit and come on out," Big Lee spat and walked toward the door. Cecil looked over at Lay as he threw his hands up in the air.

"You know your mama's crazy," said Cecil, shaking his head.

"And you know your daddy ain't shit!" Big Lee shot back. "Now hurry the fuck up!"

CHAPTER TEN

Whisper was sitting out on his porch, watching the neighborhood activities. There were niggas hustling, dope fiends geeked up, hoes begging, and little kids playing. These were the normal activities of the people in the community, and today was no different. He was thinking about a conversation he had with Deacon a few weeks ago about Lay. It raised several questions in his mind, but he didn't know whom to ask to get a straight answer. If he asked Big Lee, would she tell him the truth? Deacon was talking in riddles at the time, so Whisper only understood some of the stuff he was saying.

Whisper looked up the street and saw Deacon and Craig coming out their houses at the same time. They walked over to the end of their porches and started talking to each other. Something must be up if they were talking on the front porch. Cecil had been applying a lot of pressure on Big Lee, so he wondered if she'd talked to them about it. Maybe, she'd finally wake up and get rid of his ass because that nigga was deadweight.

"Aye!" Deacon yelled, looking down the street. "Whisper!"

"We ain't in the country nigga, so quit yelling down the street!" Whisper yelled back. They both started laughing as Whisper came down his steps. He opened his gate and stepped out on the sidewalk. He had an idea on what Deacon wanted as he headed down the street, and he hoped that both the brothers were on the same note as him.

"What's up, fellas?" Whisper uttered, throwing back his head. He saluted Deacon then went into their handshake. Whisper did the same thing with Craig then sat on the edge of the porch.

"Where's Ann?" Deacon asked, firing up a cigarette.

"She and Lay are gone to see Cecil," Whisper replied. "They should be back soon because you know Ann don't like visiting that nigga."

Deacon looked over at Craig and nodded his head. "Do you know what Cecil wanted? 'Cause the only time she goes to see him is when he wants something from her," Deacon asked and frowned.

"I don't know nothing," Whisper replied. Deacon looked over at Craig in disbelief.

"You mean to tell me that you don't know what he wanted?" Craig asked skeptically. He had a smirk on his face, so Whisper knew he didn't believe him. "You can't even pretend like you don't know."

Whisper looked at Craig then at Deacon because he felt pressed to tell them what he knew. He spent most of his time with Ann, so he had to know what was going on.

"Look, Ann already fussed at me about telling y'all shit! Y'all always go back and tell her word for word what a nigga said. Then she's mad at me for a couple of days, and it makes my life miserable," Whisper complained. Both Deacon and Craig laughed at their friend.

"Maaaan! You sound like a bitch!" Deacon yelled out. "We don't give a damn about Ann being mad at you. However, we do care that Cecil is trying to use her to get a discount on some shit."

"I never liked her fucking with that nigga no way," Craig complained. "The only reason he stepped to her in the first place was because he was scheming. He's an opportunist ass nigga, and those are the worst kind!"

"I understand both of your positions, and I even told Ann to leave the nigga alone. You know he got a bitch over on the southside handling things for him along with Geechie," Whisper mentioned. "From what I hear, she ain't no older than Lay."

"So he got a young bitch, huh?" Deacon mocked and smirked. "Young bitches are easier to control, and as long as he keeps that bitch hair done and provide money for a few outfits, she'll do anything."

"They getting money over there," Whisper replied. "The young chick is connected to this dude name Shine. Apparently, he's cellmates with Cecil and put him up on her."

"Ain't Shine a sissy?" asked Deacon, frowning. "That nigga got titties!"

Whisper and Craig laughed at Deacon and the look he had on his face.

"Yeah, Shine go that way." Whisper laughed. "And he's been that nigga Cecil's celly for some years now."

"Emmm..." Deacon hummed. "Cecil's a fag!"

"I told you that nigga was questionable." Craig scoffed. "The streets talk, and I know a gang of ole heads that told me Cecil liked fucking with boys!"

"And my baby married to that nigga!" Whisper shouted. "Does Ann know?"

"I don't think so," Craig replied. "If Ann knew, she might have tried to kill the nigga!"

"Ain't no try to it!" Deacon smirked. "She would have killed that nigga!"

"Yeah, Ann would have killed Cecil if she knew," Whisper replied. "But I plan on changing that shit. It's time for me to get my shit together so Ann can leave that nigga alone and become my one and only."

"I don't know what took your ass so long to realize that Ann wanted your ass!" Deacon complained. "Shit, y'all already got a child together."

Whisper looked at Deacon strangely while Craig's eyes widened. "What are you talking about?" asked Whisper, looking confused.

"What I'm saying is"—Deacon scratched his head for a second—"you know Lay is like your daughter, nigga! She runs to you before she even thinks to come to one of us."

"That is the truth," Whisper replied. He felt a little funny because this wasn't the first time he'd heard Deacon make reference to Lay being his daughter, and Ann always brushed it off whenever Whisper asked her the question. Lay did look just like Whisper and his mother, so he often wondered about it.

"What are we going to do about Cecil? Ann is going to give him what he wants just so he can go away for a while," Craig fussed. "She needs to tell that nigga the truth! Their marriage has been annulled for over five years."

"So she wasn't lying when she told me that they're not married!" Whisper blurted out. Craig and Deacon looked at him smugly.

"If Ann told you some shit like that, you should have believed her," Craig told him and smirked. "One thing about Lee Ann Wilson is she's a sneaky muthafucka!"

"And ornery as hell!" Deacon added. "We gon' have to figure out how to handle that cock sucker Cecil! If he manages to get Ann to sell to him at a discount, he's going to want to keep getting it."

"And that's going to be a problem." Craig frowned. "Whisper, we're going to need for you to be on your p's and q's about this situation. Ann trusts you, and that's what's working for us."

"But Ann trusts you guys more than she trusts me," Whisper argued. "Whenever something happens, she always calls you guys first. Or asks me to go get you."

"But you're the one fucking her," Deacon shot back and smiled. "So that means you have the upper hand over us."

"Fuck that!" shouted Craig. "You're her fucking driver and bodyguard!"

Whisper looked at both men and smiled. "She is my woman, ain't she?" Whisper realized, looking at the both men strangely. Both Deacon and Craig looked at Whisper with sarcastic expressions on their face.

"Nigga! You're her bitch!" Deacon shouted.

Whisper's smile instantly turned to the dick look. "I ain't nobody's bitch, bruh!" Whisper huffed. He raised his eyebrow at Deacon because he felt a bit disrespected.

"What you gon' do, Whisper? Whoop my ass!" Deacon teased. "Your swollen ass better get the fuck out of here!"

Craig laughed as he listened to the two men joke on each other. His phone started to vibrate in his pocket, so he pulled it out and took a look at it.

"This Ann right here," said Craig, answering the phone. "Hello."

"What's up, Craig?" Ann replied. "I just left my visit with Cecil, and he's up to his old antics. He wants me to bless him with money, materials, and workers to help him rehab some properties, and I'm going to go ahead and give it to him."

"But Ann…" Craig uttered.

"I've made my decision, Craig, and I don't need to hear one of your lectures," Big Lee replied. "He threatened to tell my baby that Whisper is her father." Craig looked over at Whisper.

"Would that be so wrong? I mean, she needs to know that Whisper is her father," Craig mumbled, walking down the length of his porch. He wanted to get out of earshot of Whisper because they were talking about him. "I think it's time for you to be honest with him, Ann. You've had feelings for him ever since he used to sneak and sleep in your room. I mean, that nigga stayed over our house twenty-four seven, and you always keep his ass close."

Big Lee smiled as she thought about Craig's words. "That's because I always had snacks in my room," Big Lee replied. "We used to be up there watching movies."

"Tell me anything." Craig scoffed. "I know that Whisper loves you, Ann, and I just think it's time to put all the secrets out on the table. You don't want something to happen, and the truth comes out that way. It will only lead to problems."

Big Lee saw Lay coming out of the building. "I got to go, Craig." Big Lee sighed. "I left Lay in the visit with her father, and I know she's going to get in the car with an attitude."

"She's going to curse you out," Craig added and laughed.

"Now you know good and got damn well that shit will never happen!" Big Lee scoffed. "You'll hear about a dead twenty-something-year-old female found dead on the side of the road."

Craig laughed as he turned to look at Whisper and Deacon. They were still deep into their conversation, so maybe they weren't tripping off of him. "Alright, little sis, you have a safe trip home," said Craig, rubbing his chin.

"Thanks, big bruh. I'll see you in a minute.

CHAPTER ELEVEN

It was Sunday, and even though Big Lee had been on the highway most of the day, she still managed to come home and make dinner for her family. They all met at Big Lee's house in the Central West End for dinner every Sunday. It was a Wilson tradition that started a few years back, and this was a way for them to talk business while they shared a meal and each other's company.

"Where is Ralph?" Big Lee asked with an attitude. "I told him dinner would be ready at seven."

"He said something about being late," Ax replied. "I'll eat his food if he doesn't come."

"Now you know Ralph is going to whine like a little bitch if you eat his food," Cam joked. "I say we start eating, and he can get whatever's left when we're done."

Big Lee sat down next to Whisper, and he noticed the weary look on her face. "What's wrong?" Whisper asked, concerned. "You look tired, baby."

"I am," Big Lee replied. "This has been an exhausting day, and I still need to talk to my brothers about Cecil."

"I heard that nigga is trying to buy up some of the vacant houses on Evans," Ax blurted out across the table.

Big Lee looked up at him, surprised. "When did you hear that?" she asked.

"I heard that too, Mama," Lay added. "Byrd said that he overheard ManMan talking about it with Big Daddy."

Big Lee leaned back in her chair as she pondered over this information. That was bit too close for comfort because she wanted Cecil as far away from her as possible.

"That's why I said not to give that nigga no help," Craig hissed. "He's on some slick shit, and we can't let him get any property on Evans. You know he's going to bring a lot more drug traffic through here. We've moved all of that away from us, so I don't want that type of shit back around here!"

"That nigga makes my ass itch!" Whisper fumed. "I should have—"

"Everybody settle down!" Big Lee yelled, annoyed. "Cecil ain't a threat to none of us, but I don't want him close to where our businesses are located. He's just trying to stay close to keep an eye on me because his ass is nosy."

"Even more reason why we can't let him get those properties on those blocks behind us." Craig scoffed. "He can watch what we're doing, and that can cause a problem."

"Fuck that shit, sis!" shouted Cam. "We'll fuck that nigga up if he tries something!"

"Damn right!" Ax added. "That nigga knows that the Wilson

family ain't to be played with! We'll pine box that nigga up!"

"That's my daughter's father that you're talking about." Big Lee scoffed.

"That nigga don't mean nothing to me, Mama," Lay quipped.

Big Lee looked over at her daughter.

"That nigga ain't her daddy no way!" Deacon uttered under his breath.

"What did you just say, Deacon?" asked Big Lee, sounding frustrated. She and Whisper heard what Deacon said, but she didn't know if Lay heard him.

"I said that nigga ain't talking about shit no way," Deacon huffed. "Let's eat, because my ass is hungry." Jazzy looked over at Big Lee and shook her head.

"Everything looks good, as usual," Jazzy complimented. "I think we should eat before the food gets cold. Who's going to bless the table?"

Big Lee looked around the table with a solemn look on his face. "We might as well eat." Big Lee sighed. "But Ralph knows that I like for all of us to eat together." At that moment, Ralph came walking through the dining room door. "Where the hell you been? You knew dinner was at seven!"

Ralph smiled as he walked over to his big sister and gave her a kiss on the forehead. "I'm sorry, Ann," Ralph apologized. "I was on my way and saw a damsel in distress."

"A damsel in distress?" Rico laughed. "That nigga was out there being Captain Save-a-Hoe again!" Cam, Ax, Whisper, and Deacon fell out laughing. “You always out there trying to save these bitches!”

“But those bitches are always appreciative,” Ralph gloated. “And I got a nice blowjob in the backseat of my truck for saving that bitch!”

Big Lee frowned as she stared at her brother. “I hope you cleaned up before you sit your ass down at my table!” Big Lee fussed.

“Don’t worry, sister,” Ralph replied, smiling. “That bitch was very thorough when she licked and sucked all the nu—”

“You can stop right there!” Big Lee shouted. “My daughters are seated at this table, and you need to respect them. I grew up with your nasty ass, so the shit don’t bother me!”

“Ah, Ann, you know them girls are fucking!” Deacon scoffed. “I saw that boy Pigeon coming out of the back of the lounge this morning with Niecy Pooh.”

“Yeah, I saw that too,” Craig added and smirked. He looked over at his niece, who was squirming in her seat. “You care to explain, Lay?”

“We’re just friends.” Lay blushed. “Y’all know we grew up together.” Ew Baby turned up her lips at Lay.

“Oh yeah, Lay,” Ax signified. “I guess I need to go have a talk with that lil’ nigga.”

“I think we should,” Cam added.

“Y’all don’t need to go say nothing to him.” Lay scoffed. “I’m a grown woman, and I know how to handle Byrd.”

“Listen to her,” Ax replied. “I ain’t doubting you, Niecy Pooh, but he didn’t ask for permission to date you.” Lay looked at him in disbelief. “Don’t look at me like that!”

"'Cause you know a nigga is supposed to ask permission to talk to you," Cam added. "You remember what we did to all those little niggas that were trying to get on you in high school."

Lay looked at them smugly. "Yeah, I remember." Lay scoffed. "That's why no one wanted to take me to prom."

"But we kicked it, Lay." Ew Baby smiled.

"See!" Ax called out. "Ew Baby ain't got no lil' niggas running around here!"

"That's because Ew Baby does her dirt away from the hood," Lay mumbled and smirked. "I guess I'm just too slow to do the same thing."

"All I'm saying is I need to have a conversation with the young brother because I want to see where his head is at. You're about to graduate from college, and we're all so proud of you!" Cam added and smiled.

A grin crept across Lay's face because she loved to be praised by her uncles.

"Ew Baby, what the fuck are you doing? You should have been done with cosmetology school. You're whippin' up everybody's hair, but you ain't got no paper to do it legally."

Ew Baby looked at Cam because he was always on her case. "I'm working on it," Ew Baby replied, salty. "I told Mama that I'm going to be done soon."

"You just make sure you do," Ax replied. "We ain't raising no dummies around here!"

"Alright, get off of my babies!" Big Lee demanded. "Ralph's nasty ass is here, so we can say grace and eat."

Everyone laughed as Ralph smiled brightly. "Damn, big sis, you got to put me on blast like that?" asked Ralph, and he laughed.

"You damn right! Now Deacon, say grace so we can eat! I'm hungry as a hostage, and my stomach is touching my back!" Everyone laughed as they prepared to say grace and eat.

Lay was in the kitchen, washing dishes. She had made plans to meet up with Byrd at his house later. Ew Baby had given her the package Byrd had sent, and she teased her sister about the secret romance. It contained a dub bag of weed, a pack of rellos, two boxes of Mike and Ikes—the green box—and two packs of watermelon Now and Laters. She smiled as she looked inside of the bag because he was on point with his gift. He was very attentive to Lay, and she liked that about him.

For years, she'd watched how her uncles treated their wives. Also, she watched how Whisper took care of her mother. He was always doing nice things for her and didn't have a problem with the fact that her mother was a made woman. Whisper was a force to be reckoned with as well because everyone knew he was a stone-cold killer. He made a name for himself back in the day along with Ralph and Rico when they were teenagers. Gangs were prevalent in the 90's, and they were in the thick of things. People often teased Ralph and Rico because they felt like the both of them were stupid for being in a gang. Their brother Craig was known around the hood for knocking niggas out with one punch, and Deacon wasn't short stopping either, because he'd beaten an ass or six around the hood as well.

"Why haven't you been wearing your earrings?" Big Lee asked

curiously.

Lay looked at her mother strangely. “What?” she replied.

Big Lee glared at Lay as if she'd cursed her out. “Girl, don't play with me!” Big Lee hissed. “I haven't seen you in your earrings in days and you wear those muthafuckas every day. Where are they?” Lay looked at her mother uncomfortably.

“I, uhhh...” Lay swallowed hard.

“You better come with an answer, Lay, or I'm gonna smack the shit out of you, grown or not! I paid good damn money for those earrings, and I had your initials engraved on the inside,” Big Lee fussed.

Lay held her head down for a moment then brought it back up. “Mama, I left them over Byrd's house a few days ago,” Lay lied. “I haven't been back over there to get them, but he promised that he'd put them up for me.”

Big Lee cut her eyes at her daughter. “You're really feeling this nigga, ain't you?”

“Yes, ma'am,” Lay mumbled and smiled. “He's a really nice guy, and he always acts like a gentleman.”

“Like a gentleman, huh,” Big Lee mocked. “Well, when you're done, meet me in the game room so we can shoot a game of pool.”

“Alright, mama,” Lay replied. Big Lee kissed the top of her daughter's head before she walked away. Lay's heart was beating a mile a minute because at first, she thought her mother wasn't going to believe her. Lay hated lying to her mother, but she didn't want to piss her off either. Lay almost had all the money to pay ManMan back for her earrings, and Ew Baby had hustled up on five hundred dollars, so she was just three hundred dollars short of what she needed. They got paid on Fridays, so Lay would have the money she needed to go get her earrings back.

She could have withdrawn the money out of her account, but Big Lee would know that she'd taken money out. They had a joint account that Big Lee oversaw, so she knew whenever Lay took out money or made any purchases. However, something was telling her that things might not be that easy because ManMan was a bitch ass nigga. He'd been sweating her hard here and now lately, and she felt like he might try to use that against her because he knew how much she wanted her earrings back.

Lay walked into the game room where Big Lee was waiting on her. She was sitting at the bar, having a drink, and watching the basketball game. Big Lee was a big gambler, and she liked to bet on various sporting events. Craig and Ax were big gamblers as well, and they were the ones who taught Ew Baby how to shoot craps. Ax used to take Ew Baby with him to hold his money because Ew Baby was fearless due to her home life. It was fucked up before she came to live with Big Lee, and at fourteen years old, Ew Baby was toting guns and selling dope on the low because she had to survive out on the streets. Everyone in the Wilson family had always looked out for Ew Baby because her crackhead mother wasn't shit. She was Lay's best friend and always around them, so they treated her like family too.

"Rack the balls," Big Lee ordered as she watched the game.

"Okay, Mama," Lay replied. She walked over to the pool table and grabbed the rack. She put the balls inside of it and rolled them into place. Big Lee watched her daughter as she smoked her blunt because her baby girl had blossomed right before her eyes. Lay was a woman, and it was time for Big Lee to take a step back and allow her baby girl to spread her wings. She was always truthful and honest with her daughter and never tried to shield her from the harsh realities of this man's world. It had been on her heart to tell Lay the truth about Whisper being her father and that Ew Baby was actually Cecil's daughter. She didn't know how Lay would respond to the news, but she just wasn't ready to tell her the truth yet.

"Go ahead and break the balls," said Big Lee, smirking. Usually, Big Lee would be the one to break, so when Lay looked at her in shock, she knew her mother was up to something.

"Are you sure, Mama?" Lay asked hesitantly. "I feel honored that you're going to let me take the first shot."

Big Lee smiled at her daughter warmly. "You're an adult now, baby girl, and there are some things that's going to change."

"What you mean?" asked Lay, frowning. "Nothing needs to change!"

Big Lee laughed as she saw panic on her daughter's face. "Don't worry, baby. Mama's not about to cut you off or anything," Big Lee assured her. "I just think it's time for you to take on some more responsibilities now that you'll be getting your degree. I'm so proud of you, baby, and I just want you to know that."

"I know, Mama, and I'm so proud of you too!" Lay replied.

"Ah yeah, baby? For what?" asked Big Lee curiously.

"I'm proud of you for standing up to Cecil," Lay explained. "I know you don't love him, Mama, and I don't understand why you stayed with him all of this time. It's obvious that you're in love with Whisper. I mean, the two of you have been sneaking around ever since I could remember. He's always at your house, cooking you breakfast in the mornings, and doing the things that a lover would do for his woman. Whenever someone tries to push up on you, he always plays it cool. However, when he thinks that no one is paying any attention, he goes and scares them away!"

Big Lee laughed at her daughter because she knew that Lay was telling the truth. "And I see the way that you guys look at each other. You were so jealous the other night when Amber came to the lounge."

Big Lee cut her eyes at Lay. "You saw that?" Big Lee scoffed.

"Everyone saw it, Mama," Lay added and laughed. "But for real, Mama. Cecil is not a good dude, and you need to leave him alone. Byrd said he got a chick over on the southside selling dope for him."

"Byrd sure does tell you a lot," Big Lee mentioned.

Lay smiled at her mother bashfully. "I guess he trusts me," Lay replied.

"Do you trust him?" Big Lee asked, studying her daughter's face.

"With my life," Lay admitted with no hesitation. She had a serious look on her face, so Big Lee knew that her baby was in love.

"Byrd's got your nose wide open, Lay, and I hope you're being cautious and smart."

"I am, Mama. I don't talk about our business practices, because that's none of his concern. We talk about our goals and dreams, and Mama, he's about to graduate with his bachelors in carpentry. He told me that he's going to build our dream house," Lay gushed.

"That nigga got you spent!" Big Lee proclaimed and laughed. "But I'm glad to hear that being a dope man ain't his aspirations in life."

"You know his mama don't play that!"

"My bestie did raise a fine young man," Big Lee admitted. "Does Tabitha know that y'all are messing around?"

"I don't know," Lay replied, perplexed. "He's never mentioned having a conversation with his mother about me, and I never cared to ask." A look of concern came across Lay's face. "Should I be concerned about that?"

"I'm sure it's nothing, baby," Big Lee assured her. "All men know how to do is play games. They learn early on as little boys. I should know; I have six brothers." Both women laughed hysterically. "Just take your time, baby girl, and God's plan will be revealed for your life."

Lay looked up at her mother with a serious look on her face. "I think he's the man I want to marry, Mama," Lay confessed. Big Lee saw the sincerity in Lay's eyes. "I love the way he makes me feel, and all I do is think about him." A dreamy look came across Lay's face as she hugged the pool cue.

"That sounds like love, baby girl, but understand that it has some big responsibilities that come along with it, so again, like I said before, take your time with this relationship, Layloni. I don't want you to make the same mistakes I did when I thought I was in love. If it's meant for you guys to be together, then it's going to happen."

"I hope so, Mama." Lay sighed.

"Don't you trust your mama? Mama knows she's right," Big Lee asserted. She got up off her stool and walked over to her daughter. She gave her a big hug and kissed Lay in the middle of her forehead. "You are my everything, Lay, and everything I do is for the betterment of our lives."

"I know, Mama," Lay assured her and smiled. "And I love you for always being the best mama in the world!"

"Aaahhh, I love you too, baby girl!"

CHAPTER TWELVE

Ew Baby walked into her mother's house to go visit her sisters and brothers. She stopped by several times a week to check on them because she knew that her mother was neglectful, just like she was when Ew Baby was little. Also, she worried about her fifteen-year-old sister, Dolly, because of the pedophile that lived in the house. Ew Baby was twelve when Big Daddy started molesting her, so she knew that Dolly was subject to his abuse. She always asked Dolly if Big Daddy touched her, and Dolly would say no. But for some reason, Ew Baby felt like Dolly wasn't telling her the truth. If Ew Baby found out that Big Daddy was touching on any of her siblings, she vowed to end his pathetic life.

Ew Baby walked into the living room and noticed her little sister, Missy, sitting up under Big Daddy. He had his arm around her, and Missy was lying on his stomach. Ew Baby stormed over to the couch, pissed off. Missy had just turned thirteen years old, so she knew that Big Daddy was probably putting his sleazy hands on her little sister.

"Why the fuck are you sitting up under him like that?" snapped Ew Baby, standing in front of them. "I done told you that little girls don't sit up under grown ass men!" Ew Baby looked at Big Daddy with her nose turned up. "And I don't give a fuck if he is your daddy!"

"What you come up in here trippin' for?" Big Daddy snapped. "Ain't nobody did shit to Missy. We're just sitting here watching television."

Ew Baby looked at Missy then back at Big Daddy. "Your trifflin' ass know why I'm tripping! We were just watching television when you used to slide you paws up under my dress!" Ew Baby hissed then scowled. "Ain't nobody stupid, and once a pedophile, always a pedophile!" Ew Baby looked Missy over. "This fat muthafucka ain't touch you on your pocket book or tried to make you suck his dick, has he?"

"Now you're going too far, Ew Baby!" Big Daddy shouted. "I ain't touched that girl, have I, Missy?" Missy looked at Ew Baby then over at Big Daddy.

"You ain't got to look at his ass! Has he been touching on you? 'Cause I swear to God if you say he has"—Ew Baby looked over at Big Daddy with venom in her eyes—"this will be the day you meet your maker!"

Big Daddy looked at Ew Baby and jumped up off of the couch. "You ain't about to come in my house and disrespect me!" Big Daddy said.

"This ain't yo' muthafuckin' house! My mama owns this house, and Patricia stays here for free because my mama felt sorry for her stupid ass! I don't know why she's still with you anyway! You're the reason why I had to leave this muthafucka!"

Missy's phone started ringing, so she walked out of the room. She knew that her sister was serious about keeping her safe, and Ew

Baby promised all of them that she would kill Big Daddy if they ever told her that he touched them. Big Daddy waited for Missy to leave the room before he decided to get aggressive. He reached out and grabbed Ew Baby, pulling her into him. He wrapped his arms around her and squeezed tightly.

"You must miss me. Is that why you're coming up in here acting like a jealous little girl?" Big Daddy asked and laughed. He leaned down and kissed Ew Baby on the lips.

"Take your hands off of me, you fat nasty, stinky muthafucka!" Ew Baby screamed.

"You know I like it when you scream!" Big Daddy taunted. Ew Baby managed to reach down into her purse and pull out a small six-shot pistol that Big Lee had bought her. Big Lee told her to keep that in her purse at all times because it was small and easily concealed. Ew Baby pulled the hammer back and shoved it deep into Big Daddy's stomach.

"Go ahead and make my muthafuckin' day!" Ew Baby shouted. "'Cause if you put your fuckin' lips on me again, I'm gon' plug the shit out of your fat ass!"

Big Daddy felt the gun pressing against his gut and let Ew Baby go. She took a few steps back and held it out at him. She made sure she wasn't in arm's reach, because Big Daddy was much larger than her. And if he got a hold of her again, he could easily take the gun out of her hand.

"What the fuck is going on in here?" yelled Patricia, walking into the room. "Ew Baby, why you holding that gun on your daddy?"

"That nigga ain't my daddy!" Ew Baby shouted. "No daddy would have come into his daughter's room night after night trying to fuck her!"

"Here you go again with that shit!" Patricia laughed, firing up a cigarette. "You told those people that lie, and they took you out of here. Why are you here anyway?"

"You's about a stupid ass, dope snorting hoe! Bitch, you didn't care if he was fucking me, because that meant that he didn't have to lay his big, funky ass on top of you! All that dope he was pushing up your nose and in your veins should have killed you, bitch!" spat Ew Baby. "I'm just making sure that his nasty ass ain't touching on my fucking sisters! Not that you care anyway."

"You ain't gon' stand here and disrespect your mother like that in my presence!" Big Daddy interjected. Ew Baby frowned as her trigger finger itched. She wanted to kill Big Daddy, but her mother would probably turn her in. Big Daddy kept Patricia high on dope all day so that's why he had complete control.

"You know what! Fuck both of you sorry muthafuckas! I'm about to leave, but Patricia, bitch! You better remember that I'm the reason why you're still in this house! All I have to do is say something to my mama, and she'll put your ass out in a heartbeat!" Ew Baby growled.

"That bitch ain't yo' mama! And the only reason why she took you in is because your daddy begged her to do it," Patricia replied and smirked. "Yo' stupid ass don't even know who your daddy is… Do you?" Patricia looked at Ew Baby smugly. "But you'll find out soon enough. I got a bit of advice for you, Ew Baby. You better remember that Big Lee is always gon' treat you like a stepchild because that's what you are. All she truly cares about is Lay, and one day, she gon' make that clear to you. Watch what I tell you."

Ew Baby cut her eyes at Patricia and looked over at Big Daddy. She fired a shot into the wall then turned to walk away.

"I'm gon' tell Big Lee that you were the one who put the bullet hole in the wall when she asks!"

"I don't give a fuck what you tell her!" Ew Baby shot back before she walked off into the kitchen. She went over to Missy and stooped down to talk to her.

"Ew Baby, daddy's not touching me inappropriately," Missy assured her. "I think he's too afraid of what you might do to him."

"That muthafucka better be scared! I'll call my uncles over here, and they'll shut this muthafucka down!" Ew Baby seethed. She reached into her pocket and pulled out some money. "Here's two hundred dollars. Make sure you give everyone their share, and I'm going to check to make sure you didn't cheat anyone."

"I'm not going to cheat everyone. Dolly's the one who cheats everyone," Missy explained. Ew Baby kissed the top of Missy's head.

"I love you, little sister," Ew Baby told her and smiled

"I love you too, Ew Baby," Missy replied and smiled back.

Ew Baby stormed out of Patricia's house with a full-fledged attitude. She hated Big Daddy for taking her innocence, and she hated Patricia even more for letting him. She walked around to the front of the house and started down the street. She was walking so fast and was into her thoughts so much that she didn't hear Ax calling her name.

"Ew Baby!" Ax shouted. "Damn, girl! I know you hear me calling you!" Ew Baby stopped and turned to face the direction her name was being called. She saw Ax running toward her, so her facial expression softened. Ax walked up on her and noticed that something wasn't right with her. "What the fuck is wrong with you, and where you coming from?"

"Ain't nothing wrong with me, Unc," Ew Baby replied. "I just left Patricia's house, and I saw Missy sitting up under Big Daddy like they're lovers or something!"

"Is that fat fuck touching on her?" Ax asked hostilely. "'Cause we can go back and handle that muthafucka if we need too!"

Ew Baby smirked because she knew Ax meant every word of it. She'd grown close to Ax because they hung out a lot when she came to live with Big Lee. Ax and Cam were always the ones babysitting Ew Baby and Lay, but in order for Ax and Cam to go off and handle their business, they had to break the girls up and take one with them. Ew Baby was always gone with Ax. and that's how her love for shooting dice developed.

"She say he ain't touching on her, but I have to make sure for myself," Ew Baby explained. "But if that nigga ever trips—"

"We gon' take his head off!" Ax interjected. "I'm about to make a few moves; you wanna ride and smoke?"

"Naw, Ax, I got some stuff to do before I go to work," Ew Baby replied. "And I know if I go with you, I'm gon' end up getting cursed out because I'm gon' be late."

Ax laughed at her because he knew she was telling the truth. "Fair enough, Ew Baby," Ax replied and laughed. "I'll see you later."

"Okay," Ew Baby replied. "And thanks! What you said meant a lot."

Ax winked at Ew Baby and walked back down the street.

Ew Baby continued down Aldine Avenue on her way to the house. She was still pissed off, but Ax made her feel better. Knowing that someone genuinely cared about Ew Baby made her feel secure. She was lost in her thoughts again when ManMan pulled up on her.

"What's up, Ew Baby?" ManMan called out from his truck. Ew Baby turned around and smiled when she saw whom it was.

"Hey, you," Ew Baby smiled. "What's up?"

"Shit! Where you headed?" asked ManMan, eyeing her. Ew Baby looked around to see if anyone was outside.

"I'm on my way to the crib. Why? What's up?" She smirked.

"You wanna get on this blunt with me? I hate smoking alone," ManMan whined.

"Sure," Ew Baby replied eagerly. "We can go to my crib if you want."

ManMan's smirk turned into a full smile. "That's cool," he replied. "Is Lay there?"

Ew Baby cut her eyes at him. "Why?" Ew Baby snapped.

"Damn, girl, I was just asking," ManMan replied defensively. "Maybe I made a mistake by asking you to smoke."

"Naw, ManMan, it's cool," Ew Baby quickly uttered. "I'm just having a bad day, and I need to smoke to clear my head."

"Well, get in, and let's go to the store," ManMan offered.

"That sounds like music to my ears," Ew Baby uttered and smiled, getting into the car. ManMan looked over at Ew Baby and smiled. He felt like Ew Baby was way too easy, and it felt like taking candy from a baby.

CHAPTER THIRTEEN

Lay was in her Econ 3 class, taking notes, when her phone vibrated on her desk. She tried to focus on her lecture but was curious to see who was texting her at this time. Everyone knew that she had class on Thursday mornings even though she was about to cross that stage with her degree. She'd worked hard and maintained a good GPA because she liked the bragging rights that went along with it. Her professor looked up at the clock and dismissed the class with the normal reminder that their research paper was due at the end of the week. Lay smirked as she gathered her things because she had already completed it, so that was one thing that she didn't have to worry about.

"Layloni! Hey, Layloni!" She turned around and saw that it was this dude named Uriah that she used to kick it with when she was a sophomore at SLU. "Damn girl, where you been?"

"Hey Uriah! I've been around," Lay replied. She hugged him tightly because he was her dirty! They used to cram together for tests in their Macro-Economics class their freshman year and started hanging out after class in the common area with some of their other friends. "So are you taking that walk with me in May?" Lay asked happily.

"You better know it, but I have to pass all my classes first before

I go celebrating."

"Well, I can celebrate because ain't nothing stopping me from getting what's due to me! I've worked my ass off to stay on the dean's list, and I be damned if I come this far to fail!" Lay proclaimed.

"I know that's right," he replied. "My pockets can't afford for me to go another semester in this muthafucka!"

Lay laughed as her phone vibrated again. "I'm sorry, Uriah, but my mama is texting me, and I need to answer it," Lay apologized. "It was nice running into you, and we need to get together—soon!"

"Definitely!" Uriah agreed. "Have you talked to yo' boy? He's overseas clowning, and that nigga's supposed to be coming home soon." A smile spread across Lay's face because Reed was the one who got away. Bryd probably wouldn't even be a factor if Reed were still in St. Louis.

"Nope, I ain't talk to him in a long time. You know when a nigga makes it, he forgets about the little people."

Uriah laughed because she had a point. "That might be true, but if he saw yo' fine self, he would be all over you like stank on shit! You know Reed was crazy about you, Layloni. He just had to concentrate on basketball because he signed on the dotted line. That nigga is getting paid, and he's living the good life."

"I'm happy for him," Lay replied sincerely. "When you talk to Reed, tell him Layloni said hi!"

"I will, Layloni," Uriah uttered and smiled. "Stay beautiful, Layloni!"

"I will," she replied arrogantly. "I promise!" Lay got out of her car and was headed up the steps to her apartment when she heard her name being called. A smile crept across her face because it was Byrd calling her from his car. She turned around and smiled as he looked on and smiled back. She checked around to see if anyone was out before she walked back down the steps toward his car.

"Well, hello," said Lay seductively.

"Hey, beautiful," Byrd replied. He grabbed Lay by her coat and pulled her down into his window. He planted a kiss on her lips and smiled warmly at her. "Where you coming from?"

"I just got out of class," Lay replied. "I'll be so glad when all of this is over. I have four more months to go, and my patience is wearing thin." Byrd smiled at Lay because he loved to listen to her talk. "Where you coming from? Don't you have class?"

"Yeah, I got class in an hour," Byrd replied. "But since you decided to go home last night, I had to come get me a kiss." He pulled Lay down into his window again and planted a firm kiss on her lips. Lay tilted her head and swept her tongue into Byrd's mouth. He pulled away and looked at her strange. "We ain't got time to go upstairs, so quit playin'! You know my dick gets hard when you do that shit."

Lay looked at Byrd and smiled. "Your dick is hard?" asked Lay, placing her hand in his lap. His slight erection jumped into her hand, and a smile came across Lay's face. "You must like me or something."

"Something like that," Byrd acknowledged. "I got a surprise for you. I went to the mall to snatch out on some shoes, and I bought you something." Byrd reached over and gave Lay three shopping bags.

A bright smile came across her face as she looked at the Foot Locker, Victoria's Secret, and Macy's bags.

"What's this?" Lay wondered, looking inside of the bag.

"Don't question me, Lay. Just tell daddy thank you," Byrd replied in a stern voice. Lay cut her eyes at him and turned her lips up.

"So you daddy now? I don't remember you asking to be my daddy," Lay protested. "Plus, I already got one of them anyway." She stepped back on one leg and popped the other one out.

"You know what it do, Lay, so don't play with me! Don't make me fuck you up!" Byrd smirked. "Now give daddy a kiss so I can go."

Lay continued to look at Byrd, unimpressed by his words. "I guess, nigga." She sighed, rolling her eyes up in her head. She leaned back down in the car, and Byrd pulled her inside of the window again. He kissed Lay passionately and gripped her butt as their tongues intertwined.

"What the fuck is going on over there?" yelled Deacon from his porch. "Lay, is that you!"

Lay looked wide-eyed at Byrd as both of them laughed. She slid out of the car and looked over at her uncle.

"Hey, Unc! Ain't nothing going on." She laughed.

"Ain't that that lil' nigga Pigeon?" Deacon called out.

Lay looked at Byrd and continued to laugh.

"He always calls me that," said Byrd sarcastically, shaking his head.

"You know my uncle's crazy, so you have to forgive him," Lay apologized. "Unc, his name is Byrd, and yes, this is him."

"Ah, okay! Tell that nigga don't be pulling you through no windows and shit! I almost shot that muthafucka up because I thought he was trying to kidnap you!" Deacon joked. Byrd laughed because everyone knew that Deacon would be the last one to shoot at someone. Now if it were Ax, Cam, or Rico saying it, Byrd would be a bit nervous.

"Yes, sir!" Lay called out, and Deacon walked down the steps of his porch and got inside of his car. "All of my uncles got a problem."

"Everybody has crazy people in their family. It's all good," Byrd replied. "You're spending the night with me tonight, so I better see you in what's in those bags."

Lay looked at him smugly. "Are you asking or telling?" Lay questioned. "Because I don't respond to orders." A sarcastic smirk came across her face.

"You're full of smart comments today, aren't you? I better see your ass in that outfit, or there's going to be some problems!"

Lay smiled at Byrd as she stepped back away from the car. "I'll think about it," Lay replied, coyly. "Call you later?"

"You better." Byrd scoffed. He let up his window before he pulled off. Lay stood smiling as she watched her boo drive away. She looked down at the bags, and her smile got even wider. She danced her way up the steps because she was too excited to see what was in the bags.

Lay opened the door and walked inside of the house. She heard a male's voice coming from the living room and wondered whom Ew Baby had in their home. She shut and locked the door then walked into the living room. Lay's good mood went downhill, and she instantly caught an attitude when she saw ManMan sitting on the couch with Ew Baby.

"What is he doing here?" Lay seethed with a frown on her face.

"He's here with me," Ew Baby replied proudly. "We're just chilling, smoking a blunt, and watching a movie."

"How unfortunate," uttered Lay, walking off toward her bedroom.

"I don't know why Lay don't like me," ManMan whined. "I ain't never done anything but be nice to her."

"Lay don't like nobody outside of our family," Ew Baby replied. "Have you ever seen her with anyone other than me?"

ManMan thought for a moment because he hadn't seen her with anyone except Ew Baby. "Y'all real close, huh?" asked ManMan. Ew Baby looked at him with a dumb expression on her face.

"That's my sister! But of course, we're close," Ew Baby replied. "We bad and bourgeois, nigga. You ain't know?" Ew Baby turned her lips up at ManMan and swung her long weave over her shoulder.

ManMan side eyed Ew Baby and looked to see if Lay was coming back. "Where did Lay go?" asked ManMan.

"Why? You're here with me?" Ew Baby scoffed. ManMan caught himself and looked over at Ew Baby. He put his hand on her knee and smiled.

"Ah, my fault, Ew Baby. I just wanted to know if we were going to be alone. That's all," ManMan explained.

"Ah," Ew Baby replied, surprised. "What you trying to do?"

"We just chilling," ManMan replied. He handed Ew Baby another rello and some weed. "Roll up another blunt, and where's your bathroom?"

"It's straight down the hall and to the left," Ew Baby replied.

ManMan got up from his seat and headed toward the back of the house. The ladies' bedrooms were upstairs, so his chances of seeing Lay were slim. He thought for a moment then decided to head up the steps. He wanted to see if Lay would go out with him, and maybe if she were nice enough to him, he'd consider giving her back her earrings.

Lay was standing in the mirror, admiring the Vicky Secret bra and panty set that Byrd had picked out. It was black lace with pink ribbons on it, and he even got her bra size right. She loved how attentive Byrd was toward her. She'd never told him what size clothes she wore, let alone her bra size. Also, he bought Lay a pair of Miss Me jeans with a pink collared Polo shirt, and to finish off the look, he bought her a pair of pink and white Jordans to go along with the outfit.

"Damn, that's sexy." ManMan moaned, standing in Lay's doorway.

She quickly turned around and stared at ManMan vehemently. "What the fuck you're standing in my doorway for like a creep?" Lay hissed. "Ain't you here with Ew Baby?"

"Actually, I was looking for you but decided to fire up with Ew Baby while I waited for you to come home," ManMan explained. "Why won't you go out with me?"

Lay went over to her bed and placed her underwear on top of it. "I told you several times, ManMan… I don't do light-skinned men," Lay replied, irritated. "I don't understand why you can't take no for an answer." ManMan walked into her room, and Lay looked at him like he had three heads. "I didn't invite you into my room."

"I know, but I want to know why you're so mean to me," ManMan whined.

"You shouldn't whine like that. It makes you look like a bitch." Lay smirked. "Look, ManMan. I'm seeing someone, and I'm not interested in anything you're selling."

"But that's the thing, Lay. I'm not selling nothing. You know I've liked you since we were in high school. We used to talk, and I don't know what happened."

"What happened was you stood me up to go fuck Kimberly Harris. You weren't apologetic about it or shit, so I deemed you a lousy muthafucka!" Lay explained. "You only get one time to play me like a fool!"

"But I was young and dumb, Lay! I wish you would have a change of heart," ManMan whined, walking up on her. They were in close proximity, and it made Lay feel uncomfortable. ManMan looked down at Lay and wanted to kiss her. "Come on and give me a chance." ManMan pulled Lay into his arms, and she put her hands against his chest when Ew Baby popped into the room.

"What's going on up in here?" asked Ew Baby with an attitude. She crossed her arms in front of her and cocked her head to the side.

"That's what I want to know," Lay replied equally with an attitude. "For some reason, this nigga got the bright idea to come looking for me I guess. I thought he was your company."

"I thought he was too." Ew Baby smacked her lips. "Uh, ManMan, the blunt is rolled, and I've been waiting on you for hellas!"

ManMan looked back at Ew Baby smugly then turned to face Lay. "I was just seeing if Lay wanted to join us," ManMan replied. "But I guess she's busy."

"Yeah, I'm busy," Lay replied. She noticed that ManMan hadn't let her go, but he was still standing too close for comfort.

"My fault, Lay," ManMan uttered and smiled when he noticed the look on Lay's face. "Maybe another time."

"Naw, I don't think so," Lay replied.

ManMan turned and walked toward the door. Ew Baby was staring at him with an attitude because she thought he had come over there for her. He was the one who initiated it, so why was he up in Lay's face? "By the way, I'll be over your house Friday to get my earrings." ManMan looked back at Lay with a smirk on his face.

"Yeah, a'ight," ManMan replied before he walked out of the door. Ew Baby cut her eyes at Lay then walked out of the room behind him.

CHAPTER FOURTEEN

Whisper was riding down McMillian Avenue when he saw Ax's car parked outside ManMan's spot. There were several other cars parked outside, and he began to think about Lay's earrings. He pulled over and parked because he wanted to go talk to James. He'd heard rumors of ManMan fixing dice games and wanted to know if this was the case with Ew Baby.

Whisper walked up to the door and knocked with authority. When it came open, he walked inside, instantly checking the surroundings. Big Daddy stood up and approached Whisper with a frown on his face.

"Wait a minute, patna! I have to check you," Big Daddy huffed. He had exerted a lot of energy just by getting up out of the chair and walking over to the door. Whisper looked Big Daddy up and down like he had shit all over him.

"You ain't searching shit here, patna!" Whisper spat. "So you can carry yo' fat ass back over there to your spot, flunky!"

Big Daddy stared vehemently at Whisper because he felt embarrassed and disrespected. People normally respected Big Daddy's authority inside of the gambling house, but there was something about people associated with Big Lee that never gave him the respect he felt he deserved.

"I guess your ass gon' have to leave then!" Big Daddy spat with hostility.

A smug smile came across Whisper's face. "Now I know you're not talking to me," Whisper retorted and laughed. "I'll clear this whole muthafucka out!"

"That's not necessary!" yelled ManMan, walking up on them. "Whisper is in good standings here! Ain't no smoke, Whisper." ManMan offered his hand to Whisper in solidarity, but Whisper looked down at it and smirked.

"I know," Whisper replied. He gave ManMan a five then walked away from the men.

"I don't know why you thought to say something to that dude," ManMan fussed. "We don't need no problems with him. Especially since that shit with Ew Baby and the earrings."

"My fault, ManMan, but I know that nigga's packing," Big Daddy replied, annoyed.

"That nigga's always packing, so that ain't nothing new! We know he ain't no petty nigga that's going to rob us, so let him come in with his gun because did you check Ax when he walked in?"

Big Daddy looked at him, dumbfounded. "Hell naw!" Big Daddy uttered.

"Exactly! We don't need no smoke with the Wilsons, because they come and spend money," ManMan explained. "Plus, I'm trying to get with Lay, so I don't need no static jumping off because your fat ass was feeling tough today."

Big Daddy's face softened as he listened to his boss. "My fault, ManMan," Big Daddy replied. "But you know me and that nigga got issues because of what he did to my cousin."

"I hear you, but this ain't no place for personal grievances. You catch that nigga when you're away from this muthafucka!" ManMan scoffed.

"Understood," Big Daddy uttered. "But I'm gon' watch his ass."

"You do that if that's how you feel," ManMan replied. Then he walked off toward one of the tables.

"Whisper!" shouted Ax. "Come here!"

Whisper looked up and nodded his head. He looked behind himself at ManMan and Big Daddy having a conversation as he made his way over to Ax.

"What's up, bruh? What brings you in here?"

"I saw your car and decided to come check on you," Whisper explained. "You know Ew Baby got cheated up in this muthafucka a few weeks back." He glared over at James, who was officiating the crap game. James looked up at Whisper then quickly dropped his head. "It's some snaky muthafuckas up in here, and I would hate to find out that my nieces were duped out they shit!"

"You're crazy," Ax uttered and laughed. "'Cause this muthafucka has been good to me!" Ax held up a wad of money and pulled his shirt up, exposing his pistol. "And I hope a muthafucka don't get any bright ideas, because it would make my muthafuckin' day!" Everyone looked at Ax and started signifying off his comment. James held his hand up, and a dude name Scott came over. James whispered something into Scott's ear, and they switched places at the table.

"I'm about to take a break, fellas. I'll be back in a few," James informed everyone. He walked away from the table and looked back in Whisper and Ax's direction.

"I know that nigga ain't leaving 'cause you showed your piece," said Whisper with a smirk on his face.

"That nigga probably needs to go shit because I've been licking they ass!" bragged Ax. "I've been here over three hours, and lady luck is on my side!"

Whisper watched as James went to the back of the room. He said something to Big Daddy then walked up the steps where ManMan conducted all of his business. Whisper assumed that his presence made James nervous, and that was cause for concern. Lay still hadn't gotten her earrings back, and soon, Big Lee would be pressuring her about them.

"How much longer are you going to be up in here?" asked Whisper, looking at his watch.

"If you're ready to bounce, then I'm right behind you," Ax replied.

"I need to get back to your sister before she starts calling and fussing." Whisper chuckled. Ax looked over at Whisper and turned up his lips.

"You know you like that shit," Ax teased. "You know your boo calls the shots."

"Only when it comes to business," Whisper replied. "'Cause you know, other than that, I got that ass under control!"

****

Big Lee was sitting at the bar, drinking a cup of coffee. She'd already made her runs, so she had a few minutes to just sit and relax. KeKe was stocking the bar while a few of the other employees were piddling around the lounge. Big Lee was deep in thought when Teke came and sat down beside her. He put his cigarettes on top of the bar and adjusted himself on the stool.

"Tell me something good, Teke." Big Lee sighed. She hadn't told Cecil that she'd give him the stuff he needed to get some properties together, so he'd been calling her several times a day.

"Well, the price of pussy ain't up, and a nigga can get a shot of ass for little to nothing," Teke replied. Big Lee looked over at her friend and smiled.

"You know you're my guy, right?" Big Lee chuckled. "And I appreciate everything that you do around here for me. That includes keeping your ear to the ground."

"Ahhh, you ain't got to start that shit, Big Lee," Teke huffed. "That nigga must be stressing you again."

Big Lee looked over at Teke with a somber look on her face. She reached over and grabbed his cigarettes and pulled one out. "You know that nigga is the only pain in my ass," Big Lee replied. "I need to tell his ass the truth so he'll understand that I'm not obligated to do shit for him."

"Only you know what's best for you, baby. This old man has seen a lot and done a lot in my days. I appreciate you for taking such good care of me. Instead of killing me and throwing me in the river, you took me in and showed me mad love," Teke explained.

"I did take the tip off your finger," Big Lee reminded him.

Teke looked down at his left hand. "A part of me knows I deserved it. You trusted me, and I stole from you, but that's water under the bridge. I'd give my life for you, Big Lee, if a nigga ever tried to hurt you!" Teke declared.

"I know, Teke, and I appreciate it." Big Lee smiled. "But we're going to have to tighten things up around her before Cecil gets out of jail."

"What? You think he might try something?" asked Teke curiously. "Did you talk with your brothers?"

"Not yet," Big Lee replied. "I don't know for sure what's going to happen, but I have a feeling that Cecil is going to get out and try some slick shit. You know he's trying to move back on Evans."

"I heard that," Teke replied.

Big Lee fired up the cigarette she'd been holding and took a long drag. "I wonder what he's trying to prove by buying up a bunch of property over there. Them boys that rock that block got a good thing going on, and we have a good understanding with them."

"I don't know why he trying to slide back in over there, Big Lee, but I've seen Geechie hanging out over that chick Renee's house," Teke offered.

Big Lee took another hit off the cigarette then passed it to

Teke. "I want you to keep an ear out for the chatter on the block. I'm going to give you a little extra to share with your buddies. You know whenever we're generous to them, they're always so forthcoming with information," Big Lee explained.

"Sure thing, boss lady," Teke replied. "I'll go buy a bottle of Country Club Vodka to go along with the party favors, and they'll be spilling their guts in no time."

CHAPTER FIFTEEN

Lay was behind the bar, setting up for her shift. She still had an attitude with Ew Baby for letting ManMan come to their house. Lay knew that ManMan was using her sister to get at her, but she couldn't understand why Ew Baby couldn't see it. She was going to have to have a talk with her best friend because she could see them falling out about him.

Ew Baby walked up to the bar and cut her eyes at Lay. She was pissed off that ManMan walked up to Lay's room and didn't just go to the bathroom. She couldn't understand why ManMan couldn't acknowledge her swagger. Ew Baby felt that she was just as pretty as Lay, if not prettier. Men always told her how beautiful and sexy she looked. Ew Baby hadn't spoken to Lay since earlier, and she planned to continue to ignore her for the rest of the night. Lay acted like she was in charge, but the way Ew Baby saw it, Lay wasn't in charge of shit.

"Can you hand me the table tents?" asked Ew Baby dryly. She had an annoyed look on her face, so when Lay turned around to give Ew Baby the box, she instantly got an attitude when she saw her face.

"Why you looking like that?" asked Lay with a raised eyebrow. "I should be the one with an attitude!"

"What you talking about?" asked Ew Baby, swinging her long braids over her shoulder. "I ain't got no attitude!"

"Yes, you do! You've had an attitude ever since ManMan came to my room. I don't know why you had him up in our crib anyway. I don't trust the nigga, and you knew he was only using you to get at me," Lay fussed.

Ew Baby looked at her in disbelief. "For your information, he pulled up on me and asked if I wanted to smoke," Ew Baby retorted. "I was the one who suggested we go to our house because we were close. You ain't the only hot bitch around this muthafucka, Lay!"

Lay was surprised by Ew Baby's response. She knew Ew Baby had an attitude, but she didn't know it was that serious. She didn't want to argue with Ew Baby, because she needed her confidence now more than ever. Byrd was starting to make moves that put their business further out there, and her mother, uncles, and Whisper knew that they were messing around now, so it would only be a matter of time before everyone around the hood knew, especially ManMan.

"Hold up, Ew Baby! Where is all this animosity coming from? I mean, you a bad bitch, and everyone knows it! I ain't trying to take that away from you, boo boo, but let's be honest about the situation. We both know that ManMan been sniffing at my skirt for the past year, and here and now lately, he's applied the full court press. I don't trust that nigga, and I think he's up to something, but I don't know what it is," Lay complained. "I know you ain't letting no nigga you ain't never jam with get you in your feelings about me! You should never get in your feelings about me, Ew Baby, because I'm always going to have your back—through thick and thin, right or wrong!"

Ew Baby started at Lay smugly. "I was just saying, Lay," Ew Baby replied. She rolled her eyes up in her head. "This ain't about you anyway. That ManMan shit got me totally unbothered. If he ain't smart enough to see that I'm the real MVP for him, then he the one missing out."

"Well, what's the problem?" asked Lay curiously.

Ew Baby's face turned solemn as she stared at Lay. She was tired of arguing with her about ManMan and wanted to change the subject because Lay thought all the niggas in the hood wanted her. ManMan was just trying to be funny, and she was going to make sure he took notice of her instead of pining over Lay. Ew Baby slid on one of the stools and swung her braids over her shoulder.

"I went over Patricia's house to check on the kids, and when I walked into the living room, Missy was laying on Big Daddy, watching television," Ew Baby explained.

"What? Why was she laying on him?" Lay scoffed. "Is that nigga touching on Missy? Because we can handle his ass when we get off of work!"

Ew Baby smirked at Lay because she was ready to ride like a sister was supposed to.

"Naw, it's cool, Lay," Ew Baby assured her. "I had words with Big Daddy, and you know that bitch Patricia was on his side. She got to talking some shit about finding out who my real daddy is soon. I don't give a fuck about no nigga that call himself my daddy! Where the fuck was his ass when I needed him?" A worried look came across Ew Baby's face, and Lay knew that her sister was feeling pressed.

"I think we should talk to my mama about letting Dolly and Missy stay with your Grandma," Lay suggested. "It might be good for them."

Ew Baby looked at Lay and scoffed. "Girl, Patricia ain't about to let them go stay with her mama," Ew Baby called out and laughed. "They don't get along for shit! And my granny ain't too crazy about us either."

Lay looked at the weary expression on Ew Baby's face. "We gon' figure something out," Lay assured Ew Baby. "Even if we have to move them in with us."

"You'll let them move in with us, Lay?" Ew Baby stammered.

"Shit yeah!" Lay replied. "And since Byrd is making boyfriend moves, I probably won't be at home no way!"

Ew Baby smiled at Lay coyly. "What you ain't telling?" asked Ew Baby, turning up her lips.

Lay looked at her and smiled, displaying her gold grill. She had them on her upper laterals and one on her lower left lateral tooth. "Ah shit! And you got your grill in!" Both women fell out laughing.

"Girl, Byrd pulled up on me and threw me a few shopping bags," Lay bragged. "Then the nigga pulled me through his window and tongued me down! He bought me what I got on!" Lay puckered her lips and cocked her head to the side.

Ew Baby lifted up and looked over the bar. She smiled at the cute outfit and shoes her sis was sporting. "That nigga showing out, Lay!" Ew Baby declared. "And he got good taste! Got you Polo down to the socks!"

"He forgot about the socks, but I had 'em on deck!" Lay pulled up her pant legs, displaying the Polo sign on her socks.

"We gon' have to teach him how to complete an outfit," Ew Baby signified and laughed.

"But hol'up… hol'up…" sang Lay. "That nigga bought me a bra and panty set from Vicky, biiiiitch!" Ew Baby's eyes widened as Lay threw her hair over her shoulder and brushed it off. "And he told me I better have his shit on tonight!"

"Biiiiiiiitch…" sang Ew Baby! "Aye… Aye… Aye…" Both women started bouncing, and Lay broke out twerking. Deacon walked through the door as the women continued to dance.

"What the fuck y'all up in here doing?" Deacon called out. "My sista ain't up in here selling pussy!" Both women stopped and looked at their uncle, confused. "Dis ain't no shake joint! Stop shakin' yo' ass for these broke ass niggas up in here!"

"Damn! That was a celebratory dance, Unc," Lay told him and laughed. "And besides, I don't fuck with broke ass niggas!"

"I know that's right, sis," Ew Baby signified, giving Lay some dap. "We don't fuck with broke niggas!"

Deacon cut his eyes at them. "Ew Baby, I done seen some of the niggas you date," said Deacon, sucking his teeth.

"What you talking about, Unc?" asked Ew Baby, confused.

Deacon waved his hand as he walked away from them.

"Deacon is crazy as hell." Lay scoffed and laughed. "So what are we going to do about your little sisters?"

Ew Baby looked at Lay. "I'm going to keep an eye on them, and if we need to go get them, then I'll let you know," Ew Baby assured. "Thanks, Lay, for being supportive. I really appreciate it."

Lay smiled at Ew Baby. "That's what sisters are for," Lay replied and smiled. Ew Baby looked over her shoulder at the door. She asked ManMan to stop by the lounge tonight to see her. She still had an attitude with Lay, but it wasn't shit to really stress over.

****

"How are things going with Lay?" asked Cecil.

"Man, she ain't trying to fuck with me, and I'm tired of her making me look stupid!" ManMan fussed. "Don't no female turn me down, but she's deflecting my advances like kryptonite."

Cecil laughed. "Maybe your game is weak, lil' nigga," Cecil replied and laughed. "I guess she got a lot of her daddy in her after all."

"I don't mean no disrespect, Cecil, but she act just like her mama! Man, even down to the facial expressions and mannerisms," ManMan argued. "Big Lee got her daughter sewed up, and ain't no nigga gon' be able to cut through that tough exterior of Lay's."

Cecil thought for a minute. "Have you ever seen her with a nigga?" asked Cecil curiously. "Do my baby like pussy?"

"I'on know," ManMan uttered. "I mean, she always with Ew Baby, but Ew Baby always in my face."

"You know that's my daughter too," Cecil offered. "That's why she been over there with Lee all of this time."

"Damn, for real!" ManMan called out. "You got two bad bitches for daughters!"

"You better watch your mouth, little nigga!" Cecil snapped. "That's probably why Lay don't want your disrespectful ass!"

"My fault, Cecil," ManMan apologized. "I'm just sayin', Cecil, man, both of your daughters are the shit! Lay is bad and bourgeois, and Ew Baby is bad and boughetto!" ManMan laughed at himself because he thought his observation was hilarious.

"I'm glad you think you're funny because I think your ass is weak as fuck, weak ass nigga!" Cecil snapped. "I'm paying you good money to get at Lay! Do you still have her earrings?"

"Yeah, but she say she coming to get them on Friday," ManMan explained.

"Oh yeah! I'm surprised she ain't came to get them sooner," Cecil pondered. "I wonder what's up with that? Lee would have given her that money without hesitation." Cecil rubbed the top of his baldhead for a second. "But maybe Lee don't know that Lay's earrings are in your possession. Did she see them when you wore them?"

"Naw, Big Lee ain't see me, but that nigga Whisper did, and you know he definitely had something to say about it," ManMan stammered. "I thought that nigga was going to snatch the earring out of my ear by the way he pushed up on me."

"Whisper knows, but Lee doesn't. Interesting. I might can use that to my advantage. In the meantime, you keep pressing Lay. If she comes to get the earrings, stall her and come up with some excuse to why she can't get them," Cecil ordered.

"What you want me to say?" asked ManMan, perplexed.

"I don't give a fuck! Your clever ass will come up with something,"

Cecil fussed. "Or I'm gon' send Geechie around there to holla at you as motivation to get the job done."

"That's not necessary, Cecil," ManMan uttered. "I'm gon' think of something."

"You better, lil' nigga, or you and your brother are going to be sorry," Cecil warned. "And that's on my daughters!"

CHAPTER SIXTEEN

It was around 8:00 p.m., and everyone was standing out on the block, trying to make the last of the few dollars that were out there before the next shift of niggas came out. Byrd was waiting for a dude to come see him so he could go home to take a shower and change clothes. He couldn't wait to go to the lounge to see his boo, because he was missing her. Byrd never asked Lay to be his girl, but he felt like some things didn't need to be discussed. Neither one of them were dating other people, so it had to be understood between the both of them. Byrd didn't like the fact that Lay wanted to keep their relationship a secret from everyone, but now that her family knew about them, there should be no problem to let the rest of the world know they were a couple.

Byrd saw the dude he was waiting on pull up across the street. He heard a loud bass line beating through the air and looked down the street to see where it was coming from. Byrd's customer got out of his car and came across the street. He walked up to Byrd and gave him a five, placing some money in his hand. Byrd looked down at his palm then back up at the dude.

"I ain't got to count this, do I?" asked Byrd, frowning.

"Naw, Byrd, you ain't got to count it," the dude replied. "You know I ain't gon' cheat you!"

"Says every nigga out here trying to do something," Byrd disputed. "And since you said that, I'm about to count yo' money, and it better not be short!"

"Damn, Byrd, for real?" the dude asked. Byrd cut his eyes at the man. "Okay, man, I can respect that."

"There ain't shit else you can do," Byrd uttered and smirked. The sounds of bass started to get closer as Byrd counted the money. His customer turned around in the direction the music was coming from because he wanted to know who was beating out of control. "Damn! Somebody beating!"

Royalty, yeah, Royalty, Royalty, Royalty. Number made me a winner. Treat all of my niggas like Royalty (my brothers), and all of my bitches, they loyal to me (yeah)...

"Somebody got that Young Dolph beatin'," said Byrd, looking at a '85 Chevy Caprice Classic that pulled up in front of him. He frowned as he admired the beautiful car. It was royal blue with candy paint and sitting on some twenty-four-inch rims with gold chrome. The front grill of the heavy Chevy was gold chromed too. Everyone stared in awe as "Royalty" continued to make all the windows raddle around them.

"Who is that?" asked ManMan, walking up to Byrd.

"Nigga, I'on know, but we soon gon' find out," Byrd replied, reaching into his coat. The window came down, and everyone stared in anticipation to see who was showin' out.

"Lil' nigga, take your hand out of your pocket and come here!"

Big Lee called out. ManMan looked around because his hand wasn't in his pocket. He was getting ready to run in the opposite direction. ManMan pretended to be tough, but he was soft as Egyptian cotton.

"Dang, Big Lee! I ain't know who you was," Byrd called out and laughed.

"It's all good. Come here," she called out. Byrd took his hand out of his pocket and looked at ManMan. He walked over to a pillar by where they were standing and reached down into his pants. Next, he walked back over to dude that was waiting for him and placed something in dude's hand and walked off toward the car.

"What Big Lee want Byrd for?" asked Red, one of ManMan's flunkies.

"I'on know," ManMan replied. He stared curiously as Byrd walked up to the car.

"Get in," Big Lee ordered. Byrd hesitated for a moment and looked back at his friends. "I ain't gon' bite."

Byrd looked down at the seat and saw a big ass gun sitting on the seat. He opened the door and looked down at Big Lee.

"You ain't gon' shoot me, are you?" Byrd joked.

"That all depends on you, Byrd." Big Lee smiled and batted her eyes. "Now get in the car because my patience is wearing thin. This ain't my set, so I don't like being over here. Y'all geeks do too much."

Byrd laughed as he got into the car. "As long as you're with me, you're cool, Big Lee," Byrd assured her confidently. He reached inside of his coat and pulled out a Glock. He set it on his lap as he slid down into the seat slightly. Big Lee laughed as she rose up the window and pulled off from her parking space. Byrd watched his friends point and stare as they rode off down the street.

"So what's up, Big Lee? Why did you come swoop me up off the set?" asked Byrd curiously. He looked behind them in the backseat. "And where's your right-hand henchman?"

Big Lee looked over at Byrd and laughed. "First off, you should have looked in the backseat before you climbed your ass in my car," Big Lee informed him. "You always want to check your surroundings before you put yourself into a situation. I had the obvious displayed, but the unknown is what always gets you. Ya dig?"

"Yes, ma'am. I'm hip, but what's this all about?" questioned Byrd. "You come to put a brother on or something?"

Big Lee looked over at Byrd and smiled at the handsome young man. She could see why her baby was so in love with Byrd's chocolate self.

"Yeah, I came to put you on, but it ain't what you think," Big Lee replied. "I came to talk you about your intentions with my daughter."

Byrd swallowed hard as he looked over at Big Lee. He played it cool, though, because he wasn't sure where this was going. "What do you mean? I like your daughter, and I have every intention on marrying her one day," Byrd explained.

Big Lee hit a right on MLK and headed toward The Ville. "So you like my daughter, and that's cool… but I love my daughter," Big Lee explained. "She is my everything in this world, so I hold her sacred. I love both of my girls, and I would deaden any muthafucka that thought they could disrespect them!"

Byrd noticed the intensity in Big Lee's voices. She had a sincere look on her face when she turned to look at Byrd while they sat at a traffic light.

"My baby ain't never had a boyfriend nor showed interest in a man. I kept her sheltered, but she was very much informed. She watched the bullshit that I went through with her father as she got older, and I don't want her to make the same mistakes I made as young woman. Layloni ain't got time to waste on a street nigga that ain't going nowhere."

"I totally agree, Big Lee," Byrd replied. "That's why I'm in trade school now, trying to better myself. Lay is special, and I recognized that by the way everyone acts around her. I would be a fool to think that I could just slide up on her without a plan. Your daughter is focused, and she ain't gon' let no one detour her from her plans, and with that being said, I was wrong to say that I like your daughter. Actually, I love her, and like I said, Lay is my future wife. However, I have to get my bread up before I step to her with marriage." Byrd looked over at Big Lee sincerely. "'Cause I got some big shoes to fill. She thinks Whisper is the epitome of all men, and that's who she uses to base her decisions for a mate off of."

"Well, she's fucked up then 'cause that muthafucka got problems!" They both laughed. "I appreciate you telling me that, Brian." Byrd looked over at Big Lee with a half-smile.

"You sound like my mama when she says my first name," Byrd mentioned. "You know she's the only person who calls me Brian—

besides Lay when she wants the—" Byrd caught himself and looked over at Big Lee uncomfortably.

"Yeah, keep that shit to yo'self! I ain't trying to hear about y'all sex life. You should be happy that I didn't shoot at your ass when I found out you was sticking your thang in my baby!" Big Lee spat. This made Byrd even more uncomfortable because they were having a good conversation.

"I didn't mean any disrespect," Byrd apologized. "I had to remember who I was talking to. I don't talk about Lay to no one but my big brother, because no one really knows that we're dating."

"Why?" Big Lee wondered.

"Because for some reason, Lay feels that once we let people know about us, problems are going to occur," Byrd explained. "I want to let people know that she's my chick so that they'll stay up out of her face!"

Big Lee laughed. "My baby don't like nobody but her uncles, her godfather, and Teke," Big Lee informed Byrd.

"Lay be having me cracking up, talking about all of them! She really loves Teke because she says he's the dope fiend uncle that's crazy, and you don't want him around none of your friends," Byrd explained and laughed.

"Yeah, ole Teke is a mess," Big Lee agreed. She pulled up in front of Craig's house and parked. Next, she looked over at Byrd and smirked. "I like you, Brian, and you have my approval to date my daughter. Don't think because she chose you that you're good with the family. It's levels to this shit, and you're going to have to get the approval of her uncles and Whisper before you can ask my baby to marry you."

Byrd looked at Big Lee, confused. He wasn't ready to marry Lay, but he knew eventually he was going to do it.

"Wait a minute! I'm not ready to get married to Lay," Byrd uttered. "I thought we were riding and talking in order to come to some understanding."

Big Lee smiled at Byrd. "Oh! We've come to an understanding, and now I know your intentions toward my daughter. However, my brothers have to approve whether or not you get to continue to date my daughter," Big Lee explained.

Craig and the rest of the brothers, along with Whisper came out on Craig's porch. They all stood in a straight line, staring at Big Lee's car and a petrified Byrd. He wasn't no punk, but the intimidation was real because the Wilson brothers were several degrees of crazy, and adding Whisper in the mix was an entire situation on its own.

"Are you ready to go have that conversation? Because I can drive you back around the corner and drop you off."

Byrd looked out of the window at the crowd of men then back over at Big Lee. "I might as well get it out of the way." Byrd sighed. He hunched his shoulders then put his gun in his pocket.

"Good answer, son," Big Lee replied approvingly. She turned off her car and turned the key back. The radio popped back on, and Byrd looked over at her strangely.

"You're not getting out?" asked Byrd nervously.

Big Lee smiled at him. "Nope! I'm gon' chill in the car," she replied frankly. "But don't worry; I'm not going anywhere. I'm going to wait for you right here!"

****

Byrd got of Big Lee's car, feeling like a new man. He managed to charm the shit out of all of the Wilson brothers except Cam. He wasn't sure where he stood with him, because Cam didn't say much. Whisper seemed to be cool with the situation, and he even pulled Byrd to the side and told him to come holla at him on some other shit. Byrd felt like things were falling into place with him and Lay, and soon, they would be official.

He shut the door to Big Lee's car and headed toward his own. He noticed ManMan and Red were still standing out on the block and wondered if they were waiting on him. Big Lee had offered Byrd a chance to make some money by doing some carpentry work for her at a few new properties that she'd just purchased. He thought she was fronting for him, but she said it was an investment into his and Lay's future. She told him to be careful and to watch the company that he kept.

'Everyone ain't your friend, and when you start to come up and change your life, enemies always reveal themselves' she told him.

"Where you been, nigga?" yelled ManMan.

"Handling something for my mama," Byrd replied. "I have to run to her house for a minute. I'll be back in a few."

"Yeah, okay! I'll be at the spot," ManMan replied, staring vehemently at Byrd. He knew that Byrd was lying, and he wanted to know why Big Lee had come to pick him up.

CHAPTER SEVENTEEN

It was a slow Thursday night, and Lay couldn't wait to get off. She had on her outfit that Byrd bought her, and she couldn't wait for him to see her in it. She tried calling him several times throughout the evening, but he didn't answer. He sent her a text message, saying that everything was going to be gravy, but she didn't know that meant. She was happy that things were going smoothly between them, because he was the first boy that she ever really loved.

Lay was stocking the bar when ManMan and his crew came into the bar. Byrd was the last one to walk in, and he instantly diverted his eyes over to Lay, who was looking good in her outfit. Byrd loved the way the jeans hugged Lay's curves. His baby was stacked and should be signed to *Thick Wit It Records*. He wanted to go over and give her a kiss, but he was with his boys. However, that was about to change now that he had his meeting with her whole entire family. The cousins were even present, which was a surprise to Byrd when he walked into Craig's house. They were as much a part of the Wilson family business, but they were more underground with their shit.

"Boy, Lay is looking fine as hell!" ManMan moaned. "Those jeans are huggin' her ass just right!"

"She is looking good tonight," Red cosigned.

"I'm just waiting for the chance to slide up on that." ManMan scoffed. "She keep actin' all stuck up and shit, talkin' 'bout she don't like light-skinned niggas. I ain't light skinned; I'm just light brown."

"Nigga, you pink!" Byrd joked. "Ain't no way around it."

"Listen at this hater! This nigga always got something to say in Lay's defense. I guess since Big Lee came and swooped you up, you think you doing something?" ManMan hissed.

"That's what you said." Byrd scoffed and laughed. "Sounds like you might be a little jealous."

"Naw, I ain't jealous," ManMan uttered. "If Big Lee picked me up, it definitely won't have shit to do with my mama!"

Everyone laughed, even Byrd.

"Well, we know that definitely ain't gon' happen, because Big Lee hates yo' mama," Byrd shot back. ManMan stopped laughing for a second and stared crossly at Byrd. Byrd tilted his head to the side a little then smiled smugly at ManMan.

"Can I get you gentlemen a drink?" Ew Baby interrupted.

"These niggas ain't gentlemen," Byrd replied jokingly.

"What's up, Ew Baby?" asked Red, smiling. "You looking good, girl!"

Ew Baby smiled warmly at Red. "Thanks, Red. You want something?" Ew Baby asked nonchalantly.

"I want you, Ewwwwww Baby!" Red called out. "Is your pussy so good that you make a nigga shout, Ewwwwww Baby?"

Ew Baby cut her eyes at Red. "Uhhhh, Red… Don't play," Ew Baby spat and frowned. "If you ain't ordering a drink, remain seen and not heard."

"Aaahhh, you drove," Byrd teased and laughed.

"Like a '67 Chevy," ManMan added.

Red looked at the men, drove. He instantly got an attitude and frowned as he glared at Ew Baby. "Bitch! You ain't all that!" Red snapped. "You ain't even fine for real!"

"Aaahhh, nigga, you drove for real!" Ew Baby seethed. "I ain't worried about what a bum ass, flunky nigga like you got to say! Get your money up, boo, then maybe you'll have something to talk to me about!"

"Is there a problem over here?" asked Ax, walking up to the table. He walked up behind Ew Baby and looked over at the men sitting at the table.

"Naw, ain't no problems, Ax," Byrd quickly spoke up. "My dude just got a little mad because Ew Baby shot him down."

"My boo don't fuck with clown ass niggas," Ax replied, focusing his attention on Byrd. "Byrd, man, what's the word?"

"I can't call it," Byrd replied.

"ManMan, tell me something good," Ax sang.

"Yo' ass need to come back to the spot so I can win back some of the money that you walked out with," ManMan replied. "This nigga came in and licked the table for about three hours."

"Damn, Unc! I should have been with you." Ew Baby moaned.

"That nigga's hand must have been on fire!"

"You know it was, boo," Ax gloated. "Ew Baby, we should go after you get off tonight. Are there any games poppin' off?"

"It should be," ManMan replied. "I'll hit you later, Ax, and let you know."

"You do that," Ax replied. "Fellas." He winked at Ew Baby then walked away.

"You must be fucking that nigga," Red seethed.

"That's my uncle, dumb ass!" Ew Baby frowned. "Do y'all want something or not?"

"Yeah, we want something," ManMan replied. "Let us get a premium set up of Patrón and three buckets of beer."

"Lime juice, right?" Ew Baby uttered.

"That's right," ManMan replied and smiled. "Thanks, baby."

Ew Baby smiled before she walked away from the table. She was annoyed by Red's rude ass comments, but she decided to pay it no mind. He was just mad that she wouldn't give him any play. Ew Baby walked up to the bar and sat down on a barstool. Lay was waiting on a customer and seemed quite annoyed by it. She walked over to Ew Baby and stood in front of her with a frown on her face.

"What's wrong, Lay?" asked Ew Baby, staring at her.

"I hate cheap muthafuckas that always come in here complaining about prices. He should have carried his ass to the liquor store and bought a shot," Lay complained. "What you need?"

"I needs for Red's ugly ass to not say shit to me," Ew Baby fussed.

"He gon' get an attitude 'cause I didn't want to talk to him and gon' try to come for me!"

"What! No the fuck he didn't!" Lay scoffed with a frown on her face.

"Yes the fuck he did! But I shot his ass down, then Ax came over and pulled that nigga's hoe card," Ew Baby gloated.

"What Ax say?" asked Lay curiously.

"Ax ain't have to say shit," Ew Baby uttered and laughed. "His presence alone shot the shit down!" Both women laughed as Lay looked over at the table where the men were sitting. She noticed that Byrd wasn't the only person staring at her, because ManMan's lustful glares were peering at her.

"I wish ManMan would stop staring at me like he's undressing me with his eyes. I don't like that shit!" Lay complained.

"Well, I like it," Ew Baby replied, looking over her shoulder. "I think once he knows that you're Byrd's girl, it will stop. Speaking of which, y'all are dressed alike! Ain't that cute!"

Lay quickly looked over at the table, but she couldn't see Byrd's entire outfit, because he had on a coat when he walked in. Lay noticed he had on a navy-blue Polo shirt with the matching skullcap.

"My boo is something special!" Lay beamed. "He's throwing me up in those niggas faces without them even knowing!"

"And a little birdie told me that your bae had a meeting with your mama, Whisper, and the uncles earlier today," Ew Baby gossiped. "I wish I could have been a fly on the wall."

Lay looked at her strangely. "Who told you that?" asked Lay curiously.

"Suave told me when I saw him at the store. I was picking up a few things and saw him and Deac Jr. coming from Craig's house. He told me that they'd just left a meeting with everyone and Byrd," Ew Baby explained. Lay looked over at Byrd, who was engulfed in a conversation with his friends. She was surprised that he didn't call and tell her about the meeting. However, he could be waiting to tell her tonight.

****

Lay was standing in the back of the lounge, smoking a blunt on her break. She'd traded glances, smiles, and winks with Byrd throughout the night, but she wished she could get a kiss. The back door opened, and Whisper came outside to check on her. He'd been watching her on the surveillance cameras and decided to come talk with her for a second.

"What's up, princess?" Whisper asked, walking up next to her.

"Nothing much, Godfather. What you on?" she replied. "I noticed Amber rode up in here earlier."

Whisper's smile turned to a frown. "Yeah, unfortunately." Whisper groaned. "I told that girl she needs to call before she just pops up! All she wanted to do was get some money."

Lay hit her blunt and stared at Whisper smugly. "My mama is gon' fuck both of y'all up one day," Lay teased. "And I don't want to be around to see it!"

"Yo' mama ain't gon' do nothing but talk shit to me!" Whisper fussed. "And I don't know why she be getting an attitude and shit! Yo' mama thinks she can lay claims on a nigga when she's married to that clown ass nigga in jail!"

"But you know as well as I do that my mama don't love Cecil. Shiiiiddd! You the one up in her bed every night, nigga! You do the math," Lay replied.

Whisper looked at Lay sternly. "Who you talkin' to like that, little girl?" Whisper snapped. Lay's smirk instantly turned to fear. She didn't realize she was being disrespectful, because they normally had interchanges like this.

"Was I being disrespectful, or did I say something out of the way?" Lay questioned, confused. Whisper stared at her for a few more seconds, then a big smile came across his face.

"I'm just playing, Lay," Whisper sang out, pushing Lay in the arm. A frown came across Lay's face because she couldn't believe that Whisper played her like that.

"Forget you, Whisper!" shouted Lay, pushing him back in the arm.

"My fault. I had to get you, but I hear what you're saying. I'm gon' have to have a serious talk with Amber. We need to get an understanding about our relationship. Speaking of which, Big Lee brought Byrd over today to have a talk with us."

"About what?" asked Lay anxiously.

"You know what, Lay. Don't play dumb," Whisper replied. "We needed to talk to that lil' nigga to feel him out and see where his head was at. He hangs with some questionable niggas, and for us, it's important to make sure that you're dating a stand-up nigga."

"But I should be able to pick who I date or hang out with," Lay complained.

"That's true, Lay, but you have to realize who you are in this city. You're a part of one of the biggest families in St. Louis. Your mama's name rings in these streets all by itself, so don't play like you're some average broad out here!" Whisper explained.

"I know, Whisper, but I really like Byrd. He's not like the rest of these knuckleheads out here," Lay explained. "He's known around the city, and niggas know to step to him correctly." A smile crept across Lay's face after she said her statement, which made Whisper take notice.

"What's the smile for?" asked Whisper, studying her closely.

"Nothing. It's just that Byrd reminds me of you," Lay uttered and smiled. "And that's what attracted me to him." Lay had always had the biggest crush on Whisper since childhood, even though he was her godfather. She loved his swagger and tough-man image. Also, she loved how he took care of her mother, even though she was married to another man.

"That lil' nigga ain't shit like me!" Whisper scoffed.

"Yes he is, Whisper, but of course, you're not going to see it." Lay scoffed. "He treats me the same way you treat my mother, and that's important."

Whisper looked over at Lay and smiled. "He better treat you right because if he don't, he's going to have problems!" Whisper assured her. "Plus, you don't have anything to worry about. Everyone likes Byrd and thinks he's a stand-up guy. However, how would you feel if we pulled him into some things?"

Lay thought about it for a moment. "Let me think about it," Lay replied apprehensively. "I'm not sure if we're at that point yet. We're not even a couple. We just enjoy each other's company."

"You can't keep things a secret forever," Whisper reminded her. "Eventually, everyone's going to know the truth."

"Says the man who's been a secret for the past twenty-something years," uttered Lay. She put her roach inside of her coat pocket. "I'm going to think about your advice, Whisper, because I value your opinion. However, I think you need to do some thinking of your own because you and my mama play all day! And one of you needs to be the adult about the situation and face the truth that y'all belong together." Lay patted Whisper on the shoulder then walked off toward the door. "Thanks for the talk!"

CHAPTER EIGHTEEN

Lay had walked out of the bathroom and felt someone put their hands on her shoulders. They pulled her backward, and she felt a brisk breeze of cold air come across her face as they walked out of the back door. Next, the person turned her around and pushed her against the wall.

"I couldn't continue to wait," uttered Byrd before he pressed his lips against Lay's. A smile came across her face as she wrapped her arms around his neck. Their tongues danced inside of each other's mouths for a few minutes before Byrd pulled away from her. "I've been waiting all evening to do that!" A big smile painted his lips as he stared lovingly at Lay.

"You've been drinking, and you're horny," Lay teased.

"Yeah, just a little," Byrd admitted, smiling. "But that's not the reason why I miss my baby." He planted another kiss on Lay's lips. She tilted her head as she welcomed his kisses. He pulled away and stared into her eyes. "Your mama swooped me up today and took me to your uncle's house where I met with damn near all of the men in your family!"

Lay looked at Byrd and smiled. "You're still alive, so that's a good thing," she joked and smirked.

"Everyone seemed to be cool with me, but I'm not sure about Cam," Byrd mentioned.

"Cam is cool with you," Lay assured him. "'Cause if he didn't like you, he would have told you to your face!" Byrd smiled as he watched Lay laugh. "I see you got us twinning today."

Byrd kissed Lay quickly. "I wanted you to dress like me today," he admitted. "And you better get used to me doing things for you. I have some big shoes to fill, and I want you to know that I can take care of you like a queen is supposed to be taken care of!" Byrd looked lovingly into Lay's eyes and brushed her hair out of her face. "I really care about you, Lay, and I think we should make it official."

Lay looked at Byrd nervously. She wasn't sure if she was ready to let people know about them. "Can we talk about this later tonight when you don't have me out in the cold, pressed against a wall?" asked Lay, trying to play her apprehension off.

"Okay, baby," Byrd agreed. "Let me get one more kiss before I let you go back to work."

"That sounds good to me." She licked her lips then pressed them firmly against Byrd's. All she wanted to do at that moment was to get him off the subject of them being a couple. She wasn't sure if she was ready for that step, and it was apparent that Byrd felt differently. This was ultimately what she wanted. Wasn't it?

Lay was behind the bar, taking inventory. Friday was quickly approaching, and it was her job to make sure that things were stocked up. She did the purchase orders for the lounge, along with the other weekly audits that Big Lee had in place to make sure that she wasn't being cheated. Lay helped her mother develop their systems from some of the courses she'd taken in college.

She planned to take on more responsibility in the office side of Big Lee's empire. Her mother had a lot of legitimate businesses going, and they generated a substantial amount of money for her mother as well. Lay was a stakeholder and 35 percent partner in Big Lee's business ventures. Once she graduated, Big Lee intended to turn over 60 percent of her business over to her daughter. Big Lee had a substantial amount of money coming in on both ends, so she wasn't hurting for cash. She still had real estate that generated revenue, so she would be set regardless.

A customer walked up and slammed his glass down on the bar. He appeared a bit agitated as he looked around the bar. Lay wasn't paying him any attention, because she was busy counting the beers.

"What the fuck I got to do to get some service around here?" snapped the customer. "I've been standing her for almost fifteen minutes!"

Lay quickly turned around and looked at the customer. "I apologize," Lay offered. "I didn't know you were standing there. What can I get for you?"

The customer stared at her smugly as he looked around the bar. "Whatever..." he seethed. "Let me get a Jack, a water back, and a Budweiser," snapped the customer. Lay looked at him and rolled her eyes as she went to make him a drink. "Did you just roll your eyes at me, you little bitch!" Lay stopped in her tracks as she turned around and glared at the customer.

"What did you just call me?" Lay snapped. She put her hands on her hips and cocked her head to the side. A smug smile came across the customer's face as he wiped his mouth, amused.

"So I guess you're hard of hearing too." The customer scoffed.

"Naw, I ain't hard of hearing," Lay replied. "I just want to make sure that when I get your ass together, I'm politically correct!"

The customer jerked his head back quickly then wiped his mouth again. "So you're one of those tough bitches, huh?" he spat, smiling. "Just make my fuckin' drink, and shut the fuck up before I come across that bar!"

Lay raised an eyebrow as the man seemed to get further annoyed. Lay smirked as she walked closer to the bar, and she leaned in closer to the customer and looked at him coyly.

"If you're feeling froggy, leap! I bet I catch yo' ass!" Lay retorted smugly.

"I can't stand bitches like you! Y'all always talking that tough shit until a nigga beat the shit out of you!" yelled the customer. Byrd was in the back, playing pool with his boys, when he heard the yelling coming from the front.

"What the fuck ever mister. Do yourself a favor, and get the fuck up out of here!" Lay snapped. "Your business is not welcome here!"

"Do you know who the fuck I am?" yelled the customer. "Somebody better tell this bitch who I am!"

"I know who the fuck you are! But I want to know why you up in my shit, yelling at my daughter!" snapped Big Lee, walking up on the customer. He turned and saw Big Lee standing next to him.

"Naw, Big Lee, it ain't like that," said the customer. "But somebody better tell this little bitch who I am!"

"Again, that little bitch is my daughter, and she don't have to know who the fuck you are, because you're irrelevant, bitch ass nigga! Now she told you to get the fuck up out of here, so get the fuck to steppin'!"

"Weak ass nigga!" Lay added. The man glared over at Lay then back at Big Lee.

"I forgot you think you a tough bitch too, Big Lee." The customer smirked. "I guess 'cause you big, you think you can whoop my ass!"

"Paul, I don't think shit," Big Lee replied. "But you better get your ass up out of my shit before I bounce your ass up out of here!"

Paul looked around and laughed. "You and what army? I don't see your brothers hanging around here to save you," Paul spat smugly. "All I see is your fat ass up in here, Big Lee! You better quit playing with me," retorted Paul, pointing his finger in Big Lee's face. Paul was only a few feet taller than Big Lee and had a cocky build. He had just gotten out of the penitentiary, so he had bulked up a lot since Big Lee had seen him last.

"I don't need no army, Paul. I'm my own force," Big Lee told him arrogantly. "Now you can go on your own, or you can get tossed the fuck up out of here!"

Paul looked over at Lay who was still standing at the bar staring at him vehemently. He looked back at Big Lee and wiped his mouth.

"Bitch, I ain't going nowhere!" Paul reached inside of his pocket, and Lay came up from under the bar with a double-barreled shotgun. She pulled back the slide and placed the barrel on the side of Paul's head.

"Move the wrong way, and I'm gon' take your head off, nigga!" Lay spat sternly. Big Lee looked at Paul and smiled.

"And she ain't playing either, bitch ass nigga," Big Lee added. Whisper, Cam, Ax, and Deacon came running into the lounge.

"What the fuck do we got here!" yelled Deacon angrily. He walked up on the scene and stood next to Big Lee. "It seems to me that we have ourselves a sit-u-ation!"

"Naw. ain't no situation, Unc," Lay replied. "I'm just waiting on the word. and I'm gon' take this nigga's head off!"

"Call your dog off! I get the point, Big Lee," Paul stammered. "I might have gotten a little out of hand."

"A little out of hand?" Big Lee scoffed. "You were very disrespectful, Paul. You owe me and my daughter an apology!"

Paul looked at Big Lee in disbelief. "What?" stammered Paul.

Lay nudged him in the head with the barrel of the gun. "You heard my mama," Lay spat. "You owe us an apology, and I'm waiting, bitch ass nigga!"

"I… I… I… apologize," mumbled Paul. Everyone started laughing because Paul had the stupidest look on his face. Lay nudged him in the head with the gun again. "Aye! She's getting beside herself, man!"

"I ain't doing shit! You lucky that my uncles saved your bitch ass because I was about to make your muthafuckin' night!" Lay retorted. She was pissed off, and she was going to show his ass something. Lay wasn't a stranger to shooting pistols, because she'd shot at plenty of men who tried to rob her mother over the years, and she'd even hit a few of them. She, Big Lee, and Ew Baby went to the gun range monthly because she wanted her girls to be proficient in the craft of shooting muthafuckas.

"What the fuck were you thinking, Paul?" asked Whisper with a confused look on his face. "You know what it do!"

"Whisper, man, my bad," Paul whined. "I was having a bad day, and I guess I tried to take it out on them. I'm sorry, ladies, for disrespecting y'all. You have my deepest and sincerest apologies."

Whisper looked at Lay and nodded. Lay continued to hold the gun to Paul's head. She looked over at her mother and waited for Big Lee to speak.

"Go ahead, baby, and put PawPaw down," Big Lee instructed. Lay put the shotgun down and glared at Paul. He nervously looked over at Lay and wiped his mouth. Lay put the shotgun back where it belonged and picked up her clipboard. She went back to doing her inventory while her mother, godfather, and uncles handled Paul.

Byrd had been standing in the doorway the entire time, watching the situation unfold. He reached into his pocket and put his gun back on safety because he was going to slide up on ole boy and take his head off. However, Lay came up with the shotgun, and it made Byrd stop in his tracks. He watched as his boo took control of the situation, and his dick got hard as a muthafucka! But the ultimate was when she wouldn't back down until her mother told her too, and Byrd nearly nutted in his drawers. It was that moment that defined her character in Byrd's eyes, and now more than ever, he had to make it official between them. Also,

ManMan had the same thought about Lay as he stood watching the situation with Byrd. Lay was the type of bitch that a nigga needed in his corner, and he was going to try even harder than ever to get her on his team.

CHAPTER NINETEEN

Lay rolled over and covered her face with her arm as the bright rays of sun beamed in her eyes. She'd spent the night over Byrd's house, and the huge windows in his loft allowed a lot of light to shine through. She pulled the covers over her head and moaned as the feeling of morning set into her body.

"Good morning, sleepy head," Byrd teased. Lay pulled the covers down off her face and noticed Byrd standing next to the bed with a plate of food in his hand. "I made you breakfast, baby."

"Ah, Brian, that was sweet," Lay gushed. She sat up in the bed, pulling the covers up to her chin. She reached out her arms and took the plate from him.

"Let me get you a t-shirt," said Byrd, walking over to his dresser.

"Does my nakedness make you uncomfortable?" asked Lay curiously.

"Naw it don't make me uncomfortable," Byrd replied. "It's distracting, and you won't be able to enjoy your breakfast if you let them muthafuckas hang."

Lay picked up a pillow and hit Byrd as he held out a shirt. "You a mess," Lay sang, laughing. She put the plate down on the nightstand then snatched the shirt out of Byrd's hand.

"Didn't yo' mama teach you that it's impolite to snatch shit out of people's hand?" Byrd fussed with a frown on his face.

"Nigga, please," Lay replied. "You mad or naw?" Byrd looked at Lay then leaped in the bed on top of her.

"You and that smart-ass mouth gon' get you fucked up!" Byrd huffed. He pinned Lay's arms over her head and stared into her eyes. "Last night was crazy, man. I was about to slide up on dude when you came up with that shotgun."

"That nigga was reaching for something, and he wasn't gon' do shit to my mama," Lay spat. "The niggas that come through the lounge get on my damn nerves! They think they can talk to you any kind of way and always want something for free!"

"That's anywhere, but I just wanted you to know that I had your back," Byrd affirmed.

"I saw you standing in the doorway when the dude was talking reckless to my mama," Lay acknowledged. "You was gon' get 'em, baby?"

"You damn straight, baby," Byrd uttered. He leaned down and kissed Lay on her lips. He rolled over, pulling her on top of him. She settled her arms on top of his chest and propped her chin on his chest. She looked down into his eyes for a few seconds because she was so smitten by him.

"Thank you for last night," said Lay sweetly. "It was so unexpected."

"I figured after a tense day at work, you needed to relax," Byrd explained.

"But you straight gave me a bath and a fire ass massage," Lay gushed. "Those were two things that I definitely needed."

"I know, baby, and I plan on doing more shit like that for you," Byrd replied. "And there's something I want to ask you." Byrd rolled Lay off of him and sat up on the bed. He reached into his pocket and pulled out a small gold box.

"Wh-what is that?" Lay stuttered.

"It's something for you," Byrd replied. "Lay, we've been rocking for a while, and I think it's time for us to make it official." Byrd handed her the box and kissed her lips softly. Lay closed her eyes as Byrd pulled away. She bit her bottom lip because butterflies were dancing around in her stomach. "Are you going to open it?"

"Yeah," whispered Lay. "But I'm nervous." She laid back on him as she fidgeted with the box.

"Why?" Byrd wondered. "I thought this was what you wanted—for us to be a couple."

"It is, Byrd, baby," Lay uttered. "And I very much want to be your lady, but I still kind of want to keep it between us."

"Why?" Byrd snapped. "I mean, I don't know why you want to continue to keep us a secret! It's time for everyone to know because I'm tired of listening to niggas make comments about you! Maybe if those niggas knew you were mine, they wouldn't have shit to say!"

"Is this about you or about us?" asked Lay sarcastically. "Because it sounds like an ego thing to me!" Lay slid off of Byrd, and he sat up in the bed.

"Are you serious right now, Lay?" Byrd spat. "If you don't know me by now, then that's fucked up, Lay, for real!"

"What's the problem with wanting to keep our relationship a secret?" snapped Lay. "I don't want people in our business, because that's when all of your fans are going to come out of the woodworks and shit, and I don't have time for it, Byrd!"

"You're unbelievable, you know that!" Byrd spat in a frustrated voice. "Let me tell you something, Lay. You ain't your mama, and I ain't Whisper! You ain't gon' hide me away like a dirty little secret and bring me out when you want to play!"

Lay's mouth fell open because she couldn't believe that Byrd said that to her. "You are so out of line!" Lay stammered. "That's not the—I don't think—" Lay couldn't find her words, because her feelings were hurt. Why would Byrd accuse her of trying to be like her mother? That was the last thing she wanted to do. "Take me home!" Lay jumped up out of the bed and quickly walked over to her pile of clothes. She gathered them up into her arms and ran into the bathroom.

"Lay!" shouted Byrd. He hung his head down because this wasn't what he expected.

****

"I appreciate what you're doing for me, Lee," Cecil affirmed. "I know that you're probably going against your brothers."

"My brothers don't have a say so in my business," Lee replied. "Just make sure that Geechie is on time."

"He will," Cecil assured her. "Can we take a moment to talk about something else, Lee? You always rush me off the phone, and I don't never have time to talk to you about something that's been on my mind."

"What is it, Cecil?" Big Lee sighed. She pinched the bridge of her nose because she didn't feel like hearing his shit.

"I know I was foul for cheating on you, Lee Ann, but I'm a man," Cecil stuttered. "And I let my dick do the thinking for me. You know that I love you, baby, and you and the girls are all that I have. I'm so appreciative to you because you took Ew Baby in and made sure she was straight. Her stupid ass mama let that nigga touch on my daughter, and I'm gon' see his ass when I touch down."

"That's all fine and dandy, Cecil." Big Lee sighed, not moved by his words. "You know that I love Ew Baby like she's my own. She has always lived at our house since she was a little girl, and that's before I even knew the truth."

"I hope you can find it in your heart to forgive me, Lee. I love you so much, and all I want to do is put my family back together so that we can be great together," Cecil implored.

"I'm great without you, Cecil, so I don't see where being with you would add anything to my life," Big Lee advised. "I am going to look out for you when it's time for you to come home, but understand that I'm over this thing that we once had, so you can give up that dream of us getting back together."

"It's because of that nigga Whisper, ain't it!" Cecil seethed. "I heard he got a cute little hottie that's half your size, and all the niggas want her!"

"That's good for him," Big Lee replied and chuckled. "As long as he reports to work every day, I could give a fuck less about who he's fucking, but just know this weak ass nigga, he spends more nights in my bed than he does his bitch! Make sure that Geechie is on time." Big Lee hung up the phone on Cecil because she was tired of going back and forth with him. There was no way that she was going to let that nigga back in the car, because she knew that all he wanted was access to her money. Also, he wanted to be known as a heavy nigga on the streets, and having Big Lee by his side solidified that for him.

Big Lee was sitting at her kitchen table when she saw Lay slam Byrd's car door and run up to her apartment. Byrd jumped out of the car and tried to follow up behind her, but Lay slammed the door in his face. He pounded on the door, yelling at it. Then he held his head down and stormed off to his car. He jumped inside of it and pulled off quickly. This made Big Lee wonder what was going on, so she pulled out her phone and dialed Lay's number, but it went straight to voicemail. She got up from the table and decided that she needed to go see about her daughter.

Knock… knock… knock… knock…

"Who is it?" Lay called out.

"It's me, baby girl," Big Lee replied. Lay quickly wiped her eyes and sat up on her bed.

"Come in, Mama," Lay replied. Big Lee turned the knob and walked into the room. She could tell that Lay had been crying, so she really wanted to know what was going on. Big Lee walked up to the bed and sat down beside her daughter. She looked at her mother with sadness in her eyes and leaned her head on Big Lee's shoulder.

"What's the matter, baby?" asked Big Lee empathetically. She rubbed the back of Lay's head and tried to comfort her daughter.

"Me and Byrd had our first fight," Lay sobbed.

"We don't have to talk about it if you don't want to, sweetie," Big Lee crooned.

"I know, Mama, but I need to figure out what to do," Lay whined. "Byrd got mad at me because I want to keep our relationship private."

"But why do you want to do that, Lay?" asked Big Lee curiously. "You should be happy to have such a nice young man by your side."

"I am, Mama, but I don't want to deal with all the stuff that's gon' come when people find out that I'm Byrd's girl." Lay sniffled. "He even accused me of wanting to be like you and Whisper."

Big Lee laughed. "But it sounds like that's what you're doing, baby girl," Big Lee admitted. "And the only reason why we're keeping things under wraps is because I'm a married woman."

"Mama, I'm afraid that me and Byrd might not work out." Lay sighed. "I don't even like his best friend, and I'm sure that's going to be a problem."

Big Lee laughed as she listened to her daughter make excuses. "Baby, you're going to have to step out on faith with this situation. Byrd truly likes you for who you are and not your body or reputation," Big Lee explained. "And I think you're making a big mistake, baby girl." Lay placed her head in her mother's lap and sighed at her mother's words. "It's time for you to stop being afraid of love and let this boy be your man. He's not going to do you like Cecil did me, and you can't continue to hide Byrd like I hide Whisper. You've learned some bad habits by watching your mama make mistakes. In a sense, we grew up together, and I didn't know what to do or how to do it. However, we both managed to be some stand-up broads! I don't want to see you miserable and unhappy like me, Lay, so give Byrd a chance."

At that moment, things sort of fell into place for Big Lee, and she realized that she needed to get her shit in order as well so that she could finally be happy with the one person who had her heart. Whisper.

CHAPTER TWENTY

"Geechie, I need for you to be on top of your game, you hear me!" Cecil fussed. "I ain't heard from Lee's fat ass in weeks, so I think she played me!"

"I'on know why you just don't let me run up in one of them spots and take what we need plus some," Geechie grumbled. "We'll mask up and every fuckin' thing!"

"Do you know what would happen if things go wrong, Geechie?" Cecil hissed. "They'll mow your ass down like tall grass on a summer's day, dumb ass nigga! You need to think for a change!"

Geechie groaned as hostility crept through him. He was a hothead and believed that if a person wouldn't give him what he wanted, he took it, and he felt that Cecil was going too soft on his wife. Geechie felt that Big Lee had been violated her vows to his brother a long time ago. He knew that Big Lee and Whisper were creeping around. In fact, he was the one who told his big brother because he caught Big Lee and Whisper having sex in the lounge on a late night. They were in the back private room, getting it on, when Geechie walked in on them. They were too involved in each other that they didn't see Geechie watching them from the doorway.

"I understand your frustrations, baby brother, but you have to trust me. There are a few things that I have over Big Lee's head, but I can't play those cards until I'm out on the streets."

"When are you coming home, Cecil?" asked Geechie curiously. "I need to make sure that you're squared away when you touch down! We gon' have a party, and I'm getting about six big booty bitches to strip for us, and I ain't talkin' none of dem hoodrat ass hoes. I'm talkin' 'bout the classy bitches. Dem sassy bitches! Dem long Brazilian weave down to their asses bitches!" Geechie laughed. "It's going to be epic, big bro!" Cecil laughed at his brother's banter. Geechie always thought he was a rapper because all he ever did was sit and say rhymes. The problem was Geechie really didn't have any real rhyming skills. All it ever sounded like was a bunch of bullshit being uttered by a dumb ass nigga.

"Cecil, I got her on the line," said one of the inmates, talking on another phone.

"Thanks, bruh," Cecil replied. "Aye, Geechie, I'm about to take this call. My bitch has been AWOL for the past few days too, and I need to see what's that bitch's problem!"

"A'ight, big bro. You stay up!" Geechie uttered.

"You too! And keep your fuckin' head! I'm telling you, Lee gon' come through for a nigga. That's on my life!"

Geechie hung up the phone and sat back in his chair. He watched the front of the Gateway Lounge as he picked at his plate of food. He was at Deacon's wife Jazzy's restaurant eating lunch because he was watching Big Lee. His big bro may not want him to rob his wife, but Geechie had plans of his own. All he needed was one good lick off Big

Lee, and it would put them all in the game the way they should be. Only if he could catch her by herself, it would be like taking candy from a baby.

Lay was riding down Natural Bridge Boulevard, heading to the gas station because she was about to run out of gas. She could have gon' to the one by her house, but Byrd had been avoiding her phone calls, and she didn't want to run into him. Especially since Ew Baby told her that she'd seen him riding around with this girl named Shakey from over his way. Byrd used to mess with Shakey when they were sophomores in high school. She went away to college and got kicked out for poor grades. Plus, she was six months pregnant by the time she came home from school. Now, she had a pretty little girl named Princess that was three years old.

Lay knew that Byrd was upset with her, but she didn't expect him to just not speak to her for two weeks. She tried to go back and apologize to him the next day, but he wouldn't answer his phone. It went straight to voicemail each time, and when she pulled up on the set, he jumped in his car and pulled off, totally ignoring her like she didn't exist. Ew Baby wasn't making it any better, because all she talked about was the sightings of Byrd. On the low, Ew Baby was getting great satisfaction from watching Lay agonize over Byrd.

She wasn't walking around, singing his praises, but instead, she was whining about how he was acting like a little boy, and their argument wasn't even that serious. Lay felt like he was totally overreacting, and it was his fault that things got out of hand. He shouldn't have said that shit referring to Big Lee, and Lay wouldn't have gotten upset. She felt heartbroken 'cause she felt that Byrd was the perfect man for her, rightfully. But she acted like such an immature fool that she might have fucked things completely up with Byrd, and that was something she really didn't want.

Lay quickly turned onto the parking lot and pulled up to a pump. It was a cold February afternoon with the chilly wind whipping through the air. Lay had on a long black ski coat with a black skullcap. She pulled her hood over her head before she got out of the car to pump her gas. Lay always used her debit card to pay at the pump so she could move expediently and get out of the cold.

"Can I pump your gas, miss?" called out a male voice, but Lay didn't pay him any attention.

She didn't just talk to random strangers, and she'd rather pump her own gas. As soon as she put her card in the machine and pulled it out, she slipped her hand down into her pocket and put her finger on the trigger of her pistol. Lay was hip to niggas trying to rob and jack muthafuckas when they're trying to get gas, and she was driving Big Lee's Jaguar, so she really was nervous about a nigga trying to slide up on her.

"Damn! You just gon' ignore me like that! That's cold blooded, Layloni Wilson!" said the man. Lay turned around to see who was talking to her because he called her by her full government name. She looked over in the man's direction and smiled when she saw a blast from her past.

"Oh my God! Where have you been?" Lay smiled, placing her pump into her gas tank. She started it then walked over to him. "Hey, stranger!"

"Hey, you," said Reed, an old college friend of Lay's. Lay wrapped her arms around his waist and squeezed tightly. He used to be in a couple of her classes before he graduated two years ago, and they had a little thing going on. "Damn, you feel good!"

"And you smell good as usual," Lay countered. She pulled away from Reed and smiled bashfully. "How are you?"

"I'm well," Reed replied. "However, I'm even better now that I've seen you. Let me get your number before you disappear on me again."

Lay looked at him confused. "What are you talking about? Everyone knows where to find me in the Lou," Lay replied arrogantly. "Remember, my mother owns the lounge that sits on the corner of MLK and Billups Avenue."

"That's right! What's the name? Don't tell me!" Reed insisted. "The Gateway! The Gateway Lounge! Oh, and how are your crazy ass uncles?" Reed continued to laugh as he pulled Lay into him.

"They're crazy as ever," Lay replied and chuckled. Reed stood at least three feet over Lay, and she had to lean back to look up at him. He played basketball overseas in Spain, and he left before he had a chance to take Lay out on an official date. They used to study together in a study group and hung out at his dorm room, but they never went out on a formal date, because Lay was afraid to go out with him. Her mother and uncles always treated her like she was a little girl, and she didn't want Reed to have the uncomfortable Wilson experience.

"I want to take you out while I'm in town, lady," Reed informed her. "You know I miss my kitty cat!" Reed leaned down and kissed Lay on the lips. Her eyes widened as she stared blankly up at him, and he noticed the frazzled look on Lay's face. "Did I overstep my bounds? Do you have a man? Not that I even care."

A warm smile crept across Lay's face because she didn't know what was going on between her and Byrd. They'd never made it official and got into an argument when Byrd tried to make her his gal.

"I'm in a situation, but it ain't nothing serious," Lay offered.

"So that means I can get some of my kitty cat while I'm here?" Reed asked lustfully.

"This muthafucka a full cat now!" Lay shot back. "It's all tiger status, patna!" They both laughed as Reed hugged Lay tightly. The gas pumped jumped, letting Lay know that her tank was full. "Well, my tank's full, so you know what that mean."

"Give me your number before you go," Reed insisted. "I want to take you out to dinner tonight."

"Aaahhh, that's sweet, but I have to be at work by six," Lay mentioned and frowned.

"You mean to tell me that the little princess has a job?" Reed scoffed. Lay rolled her eyes at him.

"I beg your pardon! I still work at the lounge," she replied. "Now you know my mama ain't gon' let me work nowhere else. She's always going to keep her baby girl close."

"How is your mama?" asked Reed happily. "That lady is something else, and where's Ew Baby! Don't tell me she's got about four kids and four baby daddies."

Lay fell out laughing because Ew Baby had run through half of the basketball team before Lay had decided to give Reed some pussy. "She's good," Lay replied and laughed. "And she still doesn't have any kids! She's going to cosmetology school to get her license to do hair."

"Do y'all still live in that same apartment?" Reed recalled.

"Yeap!" Lay's text message signal went off, and it reminded her that she needed to get going. "Let me give you my number so I can go. I was only supposed to be getting gas, and my mama probably is cursing me out as we speak."

Reed laughed because he remembered Big Lee well. She cursed him out the first time they met because Reed had brought Lay home way past her curfew the next morning. Lay made up some lie about falling asleep while they were studying, but Big Lee wasn't stupid by a long shot.

"What's the number?" asked Reed with his phone in his hand. Lay uttered off her phone number and smiled coyly at Reed. "I'll call you later." Reed bent down and kissed Lay again. This time, he let it linger for a few seconds, then he pulled away. "Damn, your lips are still sweet as honey!"

"It's my lip gloss," Lay quipped. "You know it be poppin'!"

Reed laughed as he pushed Lay away jokingly. Lay ran over to her car and pulled the pump out of her tank. She hung it up and closed her gas cap quickly. The wind was whippin', and she was cold as hell!

Lay jumped in her car and started it up. The doors locked as she put on her seatbelt. She reached into her pocket and pulled out her pistol, setting it down in the console. Next, she pulled out her phone to check her text message. Surprisingly, it was a message from Byrd. Lay quickly hit the button and put the code into her iPhone. She had been waiting for a message from Byrd for weeks, and she was happy that he finally decided to text her.

Text Message (Bryd): *So that's why you don't want anyone to know that we're together. You meeting niggas across town at gas stations and shit! Man, fuck you, Lay!*

Lay sat paralyzed as she stared at the message. She looked up from her phone and looked around the gas station parking lot. She didn't see Byrd's car, but she noticed ManMan's Tahoe sitting in one of the parking spaces. She knew that he was the one who ran his mouth, but she had no way to prove it. Byrd just might be in the truck, but she couldn't risk walking up to it. ManMan had no idea that Byrd was her man, not unless he decided to tell his best friend, which she doubted. Lay sat there for a minute, contemplating what to do. A sudden attitude came across her as Ew Baby's voice came ringing through her ears. *'That nigga been riding around with that skanky ass bitch, Shakey'*, Lay thought. Lay hit the comment space and started her message back to Byrd.

Text Message (Lay): *At least I have enough respect to meet who ever somewhere outside the hood. You riding hood rat ass bitches around in your shit for everyone to see! So you can't afford to say shit to me!*

Lay had an attitude because it wasn't what Byrd thought. Reed caught Lay off guard, but was it so bad that she ran into him? Byrd seemed to move on quickly, so why shouldn't she explore other options. She felt that they had a little misunderstanding, and Byrd overreacted to the nineteenth power! Reed was a pro athlete, even if it was overseas. She used to like being with him because he was the opposite of the street niggas she was used to being around. He was a county nigga, and her folks felt that county niggas were lames. Reed came from an affluent family, so he never had to struggle growing up. Neither did Lay, but they were from two different worlds.

Lay was looking forward to hearing from Reed since Byrd had an attitude. He would be a much-needed distraction from Byrd, and that was something that Lay obviously needed. Besides, Byrd drew first blood, and she was going to show him how the game was actually played!

CHAPTER TWENTY-ONE

"You sure Byrd ain't around?" Lay questioned, checking her surroundings.

"I'm sure, Lay, damn!" Ew Baby fussed. "I told you I saw his car parked up at Ranken."

Lay continued up the path to ManMan's house because she was going to get her earrings. She'd been had the money, but she was trying to avoid running into Byrd, so she never went to get them. Another week had passed, and it felt like they were at war.

He was purposefully bringing Shakey into the lounge to make Lay jealous. She wanted her mama to put them both out, but Big Lee laughed at her daughter. She told Lay to let the silly muthafucka keep spending up his money with them. Big Lee even took a separate glass and put all the money that Byrd spent at the lounge in it. She told Lay that it was her tips for putting up with the bullshit without acting a fool. Byrd would always send a hefty tip when he paid for his drinks as a way of showing Lay some love. He still wanted to look out for Lay even though he was mad at her and would tell the waitresses to give it to her deliberately. He'd seen her with that nigga ManMan said she was kissing on at the gas station, so he figured that that nigga was cool with being her fucking shadow man.

"It shouldn't take us that long to get my earrings," said Lay, knocking on the door.

"I hope so because I got to study for school," Ew Baby whined. "I'm almost done, and I have to get ready to take the State Boards."

"I'm so proud of you, Ew Baby," Lay praised. The door came open, and ManMan stood in front of Lay, smiling like a Cheshire cat. "What the fuck you smiling like that for? You look like a creep!"

"A sexy creep," mumbled Ew Baby.

Lay looked back at her sister and rolled her eyes. "Any way! Can we come in or naw? I came to get my earrings." Lay scoffed.

"I, huh..." ManMan stuttered. "I'm on my way out. You gon' have to wait until I come back."

Lay frowned up her face. "Nigga, what!" she snapped. "You better walk your long ass back up into that house and get my shit! I got your money!"

"You was supposed to come holla at me weeks ago," ManMan complained. "I ain't got time to be arguing with you, Lay! Either you gon' come back to get them, or I'm gon' keep them muthafuckas!"

Lay narrowed her eyes at him, and her jaws tightened. She was pissed off because she knew that ManMan was bullshitting with her. "I'll be back, ole bitch ass nigga! But you better have my earrings, or it's like that!" Lay snapped. She turned on her heels and stormed off to her car. Ew Baby stood, smiling at ManMan while he watched Lay get into her car.

"Ain't you going with your girl?" asked ManMan blankly. "She's about to leave you."

"She ain't going nowhere without me," Ew Baby declared and smacked her lips. Lay put her car in drive and pulled off down the street. Ew Baby whirled around and stared in disbelief as Lay whipped a U-turn in the middle of the street and pulled back up in front of ManMan's apartment.

"Bring your ass on, Ew Baby!" Lay shouted.

"Damn, Lay! You ain't have to leave me!" Ew Baby fussed. She walked off toward the car as Lay glared angrily at ManMan. "That was totally embarrassing!"

"You should have brought your ass on when I walked off," Lay snapped. Ew Baby got into the car and slammed her door. Lay glared over at Ew Baby then pulled off but not before she made her back tires spin on her uncle Cam's Camaro. ManMan stared lustfully because Lay's aggressive behavior was turning him on. He wanted to get with Lay in the worse way, and he was going to try everything he could to pull his object of desire.

****

Lay was at the end of her shift, and everyone seemed to have enjoyed themselves. Big Lee had a Valentine's Day Party at the lounge, and she had made a special dinner for her customers. She gave away single red rose and boxes of chocolates to the women, and all couples got complimentary champagne. Lay was bummed out because she had planned a romantic evening for her and Byrd over a month ago. She couldn't get her money back on the suite she rented, so she figured she'd go there after work and cry her little eyes out.

Lay walked to the back of the lounge to get some supplies for the bar. She told her mother that she'd close up and have Teke make sure she got to her car safely. There wasn't anyone sitting at the bar when she went to go get the stuff. However, when she came back into the room, there was a man sitting at the bar, being hidden by a huge bundle of balloons. Lay scoffed because she was about to lock the doors, and the last thing she wanted to do was wait on a customer.

"I'm sorry, but we're closing," Lay called out.

"That's good because I came to swoop you up any way," said the man. He moved the balloons, and Reed peeked out with a bright smile on his face. "Hey, you!"

"Hey, you," Lay replied in a chipper voice and smiled. "What are you doing here?"

"Well, I didn't have a Valentine, and I remembered this girl from around the way that's in a situation," Reed mocked.

"Ha… ha… ha… ha… ha…" Lay said sarcastically. "You got jokes, I see."

"And balloons! I have balloons for you," Reed countered. He got up off his stool and walked over to Lay. He handed her the balloons and smiled then kissed her softly on the lips. "Happy Valentine's Day, beautiful."

Lay smiled as she took the balloons from Reed. "Happy Valentine's Day." Lay smiled. She rose up on her tiptoes then planted another kiss on Reed's lips. He lifted Lay off her feet and held her up firmly against his chest. Lay wrapped her legs around his waist as she welcomed his thick tongue into her mouth. "Wait a minute." Lay moaned, pulling away from Reed. "I have to finish closing up, but I have an awesome surprise for you!"

"As long as it involves you getting butt naked, then I'm with it!" Reed quipped.

"Oh! We're going to get naked," Lay added, raising an eyebrow. "Give me about twenty minutes, and I'll be ready to go. Lay got down off Reed and walked over to the bar. She tied the balloons around one of the stools then went back to closing the lounge. Even though Reed wasn't the person she'd hope to spend her night with, she'd take his company by default because his dick was big, and he his tongue was mighty!

Lay had finished her work and quickly grabbed her coat. She was ready to sip on champagne in a Jacuzzi with Reed and forget about what's his name for a while. She turned off the main lights and left the hanging ones on. Reed finished his drink as Lay came from behind the bar and smiled at her warmly.

"Teke, I'm leaving!" shouted Lay, grabbing her balloons.

"Wait a minute, Lay!" Teke yelled back. "I got something for you!"

"I'll get it from you tomorrow, Teke. I have someone waiting for me!" Lay yelled. "See you later!" Lay waved her hand at Reed to come on. He walked up behind her, wrapping his arms around her waist. He kissed her shoulder then pulled her close to him.

"I can't wait to feel you." Reed moaned. "It's been a long time, Layloni, and I miss you so much!"

"I'm gon' give you some pussy, Reed. You don't have to talk up on it," said Lay smugly.

"I'm serious, Lay. I've missed you a lot," Reed admitted. "It can get kind of lonely overseas when all of your loved ones are millions of miles away from you."

"I can imagine," Lay replied. "I need for you to step outside so I can set the alarm." Reed kissed her lips softly then stepped outside the door. Lay quickly ran back behind the bar and went over to the safe. She put the combination into the keypad and opened the hatch. She didn't want to chance anything by letting Reed know about the safe. She'd never thought to do this with Byrd, but he was someone she trusted.

"Let's go." Lay beamed, walking out of the lounge. She put her key into the lock and turned it, securely locking the door. "Are you ready for some of this good stuff?"

"I was born ready," Reed replied, biting his bottom lip. He grabbed Lay by her coat and pulled her into him. He leaned down and kissed her lips as Byrd sat across the street, watching them from his car. He planned to make up with Lay because he missed her terribly. He was just riding around with Shakey to make Lay jealous. He had sent a bouquet of white roses along with a huge teddy bear and a heart-shaped box of chocolates into the lounge with Teke. He was supposed to give it to her right before she walked out of the door; then Byrd was going to be outside waiting for her to tell her how he felt. However, when Reed came out and stood in front of the lounge, Byrd's face went from happy to angry instantly. He had been stalking Lay and hadn't noticed anyone coming or going from her apartment. Byrd wondered who this new nigga was that seemed to have Lay's nose wide open. He remembered being the only one that Lay ever kissed or showed any type of affections to. Was Lay being sneaky behind his back all of this time and fucking around with another nigga? Was that why she wanted to keep him like the best-kept secret?

Lay was headed toward Reed's car when she noticed a car parked over on her uncle's lot. She looked behind Reed and noticed it was Byrd's Challenger, but what was it doing right there? She wondered was he there to get her, but he had all day to say something to her. Technically, Valentine's Day was over, and he picked a fine time to show up.

"Hey, I need to run to my house for a second." Lay moaned. "Can you go ahead and drive around there, and I will follow you in my car."

"Sure thing, Lay," Reed replied. He walked her to her car and helped put the balloons inside. Lay sat and waited for Reed to pull up alongside of her, and he was looking good in his G-Wagon. He let his window down and smiled at Lay as she rolled hers down.

"Gone around. Here I come." She smiled. Reed pulled off and hit the corner. The lights on Byrd's car went from dim to fully on, and they shone inside of her car, damn near blinding her. Lay put her arm up to shield her eyes from the bright lights. She put her car in drive then swung around on the parking lot of the store. She jumped out of her car and walked toward Byrd's vehicle. She knocked on his window, but he pulled out of his parking spot and drove off, leaving Lay standing there with a blank expression on her face. She wondered what the fuck was up with that, but she knew what it was without a second thought. Byrd had watched Reed's display of affection toward her, and it must have really pissed him off. However, Lay was too annoyed to even care. A nigga couldn't take it when a chick gave them a bite from the plate they were serving!

CHAPTER TWENTY-TWO

"Good morning, sleepy head," Whisper moaned, rubbing up Amber's thigh. "Did you sleep well?"

"I slept perfectly," Amber replied. She rolled over to face Whisper. "I got pretty drunk last night." She giggled as she nestled her head into his chest.

"Yes, you did," he agreed and smirked. "And you slept the entire evening away."

"I'm sorry, baby," she replied. "I know you had a romantic evening planned for us, and I messed it up."

"That's okay," Whisper assured her. "I made the best of the evening anyway." Whisper and Big Lee had spent the morning and afternoon together to celebrate Valentine's Day. They exchanged gifts and had a romantic breakfast at the Four Seasons, then Whisper took Big Lee to the movies to enjoy a film before she had to get to work.

"What did you do last night?" asked Amber curiously.

"I watched television and caught up on some paperwork that I needed to do," Whisper replied.

"Paperwork? I never pegged you for the paperwork type," said Amber smugly. She kissed Whisper's chest then climbed out of the bed. He stared at her with a bit of an attitude because he wanted to know what the fuck she meant by that statement.

"What do you mean by that?" Whisper asked defensively. Amber looked back at him as she slid on one of his t-shirts.

"Huh? What are you talking about Whisper?" she quaked. "I'm just saying, babe. You don't strike me as the paperwork type."

"Oh, I see," Whisper replied nonchalantly. "I guess you think I ride around all day selling dope."

"Not all day, but you do, babe," Amber replied sarcastically. "And you're good at what you do." Amber walked up to the bed and stared at Whisper curiously. "Babe, I don't want to argue with you this morning. I have a splitting headache, and I have a meeting with this man who wants me to do a few ads for him. He said I had a fresh look, and he wants me to be the lead on his capital campaign. Isn't that great! I might have to go to Chicago for a few days."

Whisper stared blankly at Amber because he was offended by her words. "I think you need to get your shit and go, Amber," Whisper uttered frankly.

"What did you just say to me, Jamal?" Amber scoffed.

"You heard me, Amber," Whisper replied. He got up out of the bed and walked toward Amber. "You don't know shit about me, and that's sad, considering we've been messing around for two years now. I guess Big Lee was right when she said all you wanted was my money."

Amber's face drew up into a frown. "What does that fat bitch know?" Amber snapped. "All she does is pull your strings like a little puppet, and you come running each and every time she calls."

"At least I know she has my back! She knows that I know how to do paperwork," Whisper shot back. "Look, Amber. I ain't been feeling you for a while now. I liked hanging out with you because you can be a lot of fun when you're not being a bitch. However, I'm in love with someone else, and I don't see why we have to keep faking and shit."

Amber stared at Whisper vehemently. "What the fuck you mean you're in love with someone else?" Amber shouted in outrage. "Who the fuck is she? Because I know she's not as fine as me! You're lucky I even gave you the time of day, Jamal!"

"Bitch, don't flatter yourself!" Whisper retorted. "I've had bitches that look ten times better than your broke ass! You's a hoe, trick, jump off, scallywag ass bitch, looking for the hippest nigga to take care of you! Now I ain't gon' lie. The sex is cool, but your personality stinks, and so does your character!"

"I-I-I..." stuttered Amber. She was lost for words because Whisper had never talked to her in such a manner. "How could you say those things to me? I truly love you, Jamal!"

"Bitch, you don't love me," he mocked and laughed. "You loved riding around in my cars and spending my money. Well, I guess you're going to have to find a new sucka to take care of you now. So gather your shit so I can drop your ass off at home. Make sure you take all of your shit up out of here, or I'll be donating it to one of the little girls that live on the block!"

Tears welled up in Amber's eyes because she knew that this was the last thing she wanted to happen. Whisper took damn good care of her, and she knew that no other man would shell her out cash and not expect her to sleep with him every night.

"Can we talk about this?" Amber stammered. "I'm sorry if I offended you. I think it's the hangover." She put her hand up against her forehead. "I have a headache. Do you have some aspirin?"

"Yeah, I got some aspirin," Whisper seethed. "I'll get you them while you pack your shit!"

****

Big Lee walked into the lounge and noticed a large teddy bear sitting on one of the stools along with a bouquet of roses and a box of candy. She frowned at the items because she wondered whose shit it was left in the bar. She walked over and put her things down on top of the counter. She slid onto her favorite seat and pulled her cigarettes out of her purse.

"Whose shit is this, Teke?" Big Lee hissed. "I thought Lay was supposed to clean up the lounge last night."

"That's Lay's stuff," Teke replied. "Byrd sent it in here for Lay, but I was too late to give it to her."

Big Lee smiled as she looked at the flowers. "That boy's trying to win my baby's heart back," Big Lee gloated. "He knows my Lay is a winner, and he needs her on his team."

"I don't know if he's going to feel the same way after last night," Teke mumbled. Big Lee looked at him strangely.

"What are you talking about, Teke?" Big Lee asked curiously.

"Last night, Lay left with that tall boy that plays basketball," Teke explained.

"The tall boy that plays basketball," Big Lee repeated. She thought for a moment. "Do you mean Reed?"

"That's him!" Teke shouted. "I couldn't think of that boy's name for the life of me last night. I saw Byrd sitting across the street on the parking lot when Lay left with Reed last night."

Big Lee hit her cigarette and thought for a moment. "Well, Byrd should have thought about that before he started parading that thot around in front of my baby's face. Good for Lay!" Big Lee cheered. She wondered if Lay knew that Byrd had left her gifts before she went off with Reed. She reached into her purse and pulled out her phone. She dialed her daughter's number because she wanted to mess with Lay about her lover's triangle.

"Hi, Mama," mumbled Lay.

"Hey, sleeping beauty. You're still in bed?" Big Lee teased. "You must have had a long night, early morning, missy!"

Lay laughed as she sat up in the bed. She looked over at Reed, who was fast asleep. "It was a long night, but not like you think." Lay sighed.

"Are you at home?"

"No, ma'am," Lay replied. "I'm down at the Four Seasons with Reed. I had reserved a nice room a few months ago for Valentine's Day, and I couldn't get my money back on it."

"So you was going to go by yourself if Reed hadn't showed up?"

Big Lee questioned.

"No, ma'am," Lay replied. She was feeling some type of way because her mother was interrogating her. "Is there something you want to know, Mama?"

"Well no, baby," Big Lee replied. "I was just calling to tell you that Byrd left some gifts for you at the bar last night."

Lay's eyes widened as she looked back at Reed. "That's why Teke was calling me last night... And that's why Byrd was parked across the street when I left the lounge," Lay mumbled. "Mama, Byrd was outside waiting on me, but I was with Reed. Reed surprised me with a bunch of balloons, and I guess I got caught up in the moment!"

"Are you with Reed right now?"

"Yes, ma'am," Lay replied, walking into the bathroom. "I tried to go up to Byrd's car and talk to him, but he drove off on me. What have I done, Mama?"

"Nothing," Big Lee fussed. "That nigga should have thought about that shit before he started parading Shakey's ass around the hood."

"I know, Mama, but I love Byrd," Lay admitted. "And my heart dropped to the pit of my stomach when he pulled off on me!"

"Look, Lay. I ain't trying to tell you what to do, but Byrd chose first blood," Big Lee explained. "He should have taken your feelings into consideration and tried to understand why you felt the way that you did. Relationships are about compromise, and he needs to understand that you're not the type to flaunt your business in front of everyone. I taught you that discretion is the key to success, and if you want things to be solid, you have to tell people on a need-to-know basis!"

"I feel like relationships are like selling dope," Lay whined.

"They are, baby," Big Lee agreed. "Did you sleep with Reed last night?"

Lay held the phone for a moment because her mama was getting all up in her business. "Honestly, Mama, we started making out, but I just wasn't feeling it. He sucked me up real good, but he doesn't do it as good as Byrd," Lay confessed. Big Lee laughed at her daughter. "Mama, what—"

"After you saw Byrd in the parking lot, it fucked everything up for you, huh?" Big Lee laughed.

Lay held the phone for a second then laughed herself. "Yes, ma'am," Lay replied. "I miss him, Mama, but I think he's furious with me now."

"Let his ass stew." Big Lee continued to laugh. "His ass needs to understand that there's competition out here for him. See, he just assumed that no one else was in the picture because he'd been occupying all of your time. Reed is a threat, and Byrd's either going to have to put up or shut up."

"I think Byrd's going to fold and hold it against me," Lay worried.

"Well, if he's going to be a petty muthafucka, then let him," Big Lee fussed. "Don't you ever let a man make you feel less than what you are, Layloni! Byrd don't make nor break you, sweetie! So don't you ever forget that shit!"

"Yes, ma'am," Lay replied. "Thanks, Mama!"

"You're welcome, baby," Big Lee replied. "Now what I'm going to need for you to do is come get your shit out of my lounge, or I'm going to give it away to somebody."

"Yes, ma'am," Lay uttered and laughed. "I love you."

"I love you more, baby. I'll see you later," Big Lee replied. She hung up the phone and stared at Lay's gifts. Her situation reminded Big Lee of her and Whisper's dysfunctional relationship. She was surprised when he came over to the house late last night. He was supposed to be spending the night with Amber, yet he came to her bed and laid with her last night. He explained that Amber got drunk earlier and passed out on him before they could even eat the dinner he prepared for them.

"Big Lee! Somebody wants you on the phone," called out KeKe.

"Okay. Bring me the phone," Big Lee replied. She fired up another cigarette while KeKe brought her the phone. "Hello."

"Damn, Lee, you gon' play me like this," Cecil seethed. Big Lee rolled her eyes up in her head because this was the last muthafucka she wanted to deal with this morning; and how did he get the number to the lounge? It was an unlisted number.

"Good morning to you too, Cecil." Big Lee scoffed. "What are you talking about?"

"Why haven't you gotten with Geechie yet?" Cecil hissed.

"Because the number that I got on the nigga is not in service," Big Lee retorted. "I've been trying to get at his ass for a week now, and it seems like no one has been able to find him. Also, you ain't give me the number to your hoe, so your back-up plan was flawed."

"Fuck! That nigga gets on my last nerve!" Cecil complained. "I told his ass to make sure that he was on point because you would be calling him soon."

"You know that boy keeps his head in the clouds, and he's probably somewhere laid up with a bitch," Big Lee offered. "I tell you what. If you can get in touch with Geechie, tell him to meet me at the lounge after ten o'clock, and I'll be waiting on him."

"Aye, thanks, Lee Ann," Cecil replied. "I know you feel some type of way about helping a nigga out, so doing this for me is real stand up."

"You're welcome, Cecil, but you ain't gon' keep pressing me and shit. I forgive you for being an asshole—"

"So that means you're going to give me another chance?" Cecil blurted out.

"No!" Big Lee quickly replied. "What it means is that we're going to sit down and have a serious conversation when you touch down on these streets. Ain't no sense in us running around, pretending like things are one hundred when they're not. I don't want to be with you anymore, so I'm not going to pretend like I do."

"But baby, I think we can work things out," Cecil begged. "You need to give me another chance, Lee. I've grown a lot as a man, and I want to show you how much I truly love you."

"Cecil, I'm not in love with you," Big Lee admitted. "I don't know that I ever was in love with you, but I do care about you."

"You're lying, Lee Ann!" shouted Cecil. "You need to quit playing with me! You will always be mine, and there's nothing you or that soft ass nigga Whisper can do about it!"

"Whatever, nigga!" Big Lee scoffed and laughed. "You stay up, Cecil." She hung up the phone and stared off into space. Time was winding down, and Cecil would be home before she knew it. There were a few things that she needed to clear up before that day came, but would everyone involved receive the news in good spirits, or would it cause problems within her family? Big Lee had some decisions and confessions to make because it would be better to come from her than to have Cecil running his big mouth.

CHAPTER TWENTY-THREE

Whisper walked into the lounge on a mission to claim his woman. The fight with Amber put things into perspective for him, and he was tired of hiding in the shadows. He wanted everyone to know that Big Lee was the love of his life, and he was about to tell her that he was done being secret lovers.

Big Lee was sitting at her usual place when Whisper came charging through the door. She looked at him strangely because he was walking swiftly toward her. She wondered if something happened because of the serious look he had on his face. He walked up to Big Lee and planted a passionate kiss on her lips. He tangled his tongue with hers and wrapped his arms around her thick frame.

"What the fuck is going on!" shouted Deacon. He was sitting next to Big Lee, and he'd never seen Whisper kiss Big Lee like this out in public. "What you doin', boy!"

Whisper pulled away from Big Lee and stared into her eyes. "I'm doing something I should have done a long time ago," Whisper confessed. "I'm tired of hiding and sneaking around, Ann. I told Amber the truth, and I'm done fucking around with her."

"I'm happy for you baby, but why did you just do that?" Big Lee wondered.

"Because I wanted to! It's time we stop fucking playin' and make things official with us, Ann. I know you don't love that nigga you're married to, so why should we keep playing this game? I'm ready to build our life together, Lee Ann. Would you give me a chance to prove to you that I'm truly the only one for you?"

Big Lee looked over at Deacon then back at Whisper. She wasn't sure how she felt at that moment, but she knew she did want to be with Whisper.

"Come quick!" Teke shouted, running into lounge. "Lay is out here trippin', and I think she's about to go to jail!" Everyone jumped up and ran out of the lounge to see what was going on. Big Lee had shoved her pistol down in her pants as she made her way out the door.

"Where is she?" shouted Big Lee.

"She's around the corner on Evans in front of the flats," Teke explained. Everyone took off running up the street because it was only two blocks away from the lounge. Lay was in front of the flats, causing a scene as she swung her bat, busting out ManMan's windows on his Tahoe. He had parked it there and hopped in with Byrd to make a run.

"Girl, what are you doin'!" shouted Whisper. Lay looked at him with a scowl on her face as she swung and busted another window out in his truck.

"That bitch ass nigga must think I'm a punk or something!" Lay shouted angrily. "I went to pay the nigga for my earrings, and he keeps giving me the runaround!" Lay swung again, knocking out one of his headlights.

"Layloni De'Shae Wilson! What are you doin'?" shouted Big Lee.

"I'm making an example out of a bitch ass nigga!" Lay replied, agitated. She swung and knocked his mirror off the door and showed no signs of letting up.

"Lay, you know if the police catch your ass, you're going to jail," Big Lee reminded her.

"I know, Mama, and I ain't sweating it," Lay replied. A car was coming down the street, and Lay looked back before she hit another window with the bat. Big Lee and Whisper recognized Byrd's car pulling up to the curb, and ManMan jumped out before Byrd could even stop the car.

"Bitch! What the fuck is you doing?" ManMan shouted with a devastated look on his face. Lay turned around and faced him with an angry scowl on her face.

"The only bitch is you, nigga!" Lay retorted. "For some reason, you think you can play with me, but I want my shit! I came to you several times with the money I owe you, but yo' bitch ass must think I'm a punk or something!"

"What money do you owe this nigga?" asked Big Lee, getting pissed. She always told Lay not to hide things from her. She felt disappointed at that moment in her daughter because Lay hadn't told her what was going on.

"This has nothing to do with you, Mama," Lay replied. "I got this!" Lay walked up to ManMan and pointed the bat in his face. "You better have my shit when I come around to your house later, or I'm gon' really make an example out of your bitch ass! Be happy that I only busted out three windows and took out your mirror!"

"You got me fucked up, Lay! Now you're going to have to pay for my windows and what you owe me!" ManMan shouted. "I ain't no punk either, and I'll beat your—"

"You gon' beat what?" asked Whisper. He tilted his head slightly to the side because he wanted to hear what ManMan had to say. ManMan looked over at Whisper then back at Lay.

"I ain't scared of y'all," ManMan replied. "I got some people too!"

"Don't nobody give a fuck about you or your weak ass people!" Lay snapped. "But you better have my shit when I come for it, or it's going to be hell to tell the captain!" Lay turned to walk away but not before she swung and busted out another one of ManMan's windows. He cringed as the sound of the bat hitting the glass made a crashing noise. She glared over in the direction of Byrd's car then walked off down the street.

"That bitch gotta problem! You need to take her to talk to somebody!" ManMan yelled angrily.

"You call my baby one more bitch, its gon' be me and you out here!" Big Lee snapped. "Now I don't know what's going on between y'all, but I know you had to really piss my baby off for her to respond like this!"

"I ain't did nothing to your daughter, Big Lee. It's just business," ManMan replied.

"Come on, Ann, and let's go," Whisper demanded. Big Lee looked at him then back at ManMan.

"Okay," she replied. They turned to walk away when Teke came up to them.

"The angry bird has gon' home," Teke joked with a smirk on his face. Whisper looked over at Teke and smiled.

"Don't be talking about my baby, Teke!" Big Lee fussed. A slight smile crept up on her face as well because Teke's ass always had jokes. "I want to know what the fuck that was about, and did you notice that Byrd didn't even get out of the car?"

"Maybe his feelings are hurt because Lay played him last night," Teke offered.

"Well, it's no one's fault but his own. He should have been a grown man and brought the shit in to Lay himself. Maybe then she wouldn't have left with someone else."

"What happened?" asked Whisper nosily.

"I'll explain when we get back to the lounge," Big Lee replied. "I'm going to call that little girl and tell her to stay home tonight. I should probably tell Ew Baby to do the same so she can babysit Lay's ass!"

"Now you know Ew Baby is an instigator. She ain't about to talk Lay off the ledge!" Whisper protested and laughed. "If her ass was around, she would have had a bat too, busting out windows."

Big Lee looked over at Whisper and shook her head. "I should have been more conscientious when I was doing shit around them when they were younger," Big Lee admitted. "This was one of my moves, and my baby had seen me do it numerous times."

"You can't blame yourself, Ann," Whisper offered. "She's a grown woman, capable of making her own decisions."

"I know, Whisper, but I don't want my baby out here making enemies," Big Lee complained. "I have enough of them for the both of us."

****

"You have a collect call from an inmate at a correctional facility..." ManMan held the phone as he sat on the couch, pissed off. He couldn't believe that Lay had come for him and busted out his windows. ManMan waited for the recording to stop and pressed the number as instructed.

"ManMan, give me a good word," Cecil sang.

"I got a word for you alright!" ManMan snapped. "That bitch done busted out my windows because I won't give her the earrings back!"

"Who are you talking about?" asked Cecil, confused.

"I'm talking about that bitch Lay! She busted out four of my windows and broke my mirror on my truck because I won't give her those damn earrings! I'm not having this shit, Cecil, because next thing you know, she'll be shooting at my ass!" ManMan complained.

"First of all, watch your mouth when you're talking about Lay. Secondly, my baby's a gangsta like that?" Cecil gloated. "I guess the apple doesn't fall too far from the tree!"

"I'm glad you're finding humor in this shit! I'm the one who has to pay for it, 'cause she damn sure ain't!" ManMan retorted.

"Calm down, youngster. I'll have Geechie take care of your

windows," Cecil replied. "And you can go ahead and give Lay her earrings back. I talked with her mama, and Big Lee's going to deliver on her word. I've been trying to get in contact with Geechie, but his ass ain't answering his phone."

"Geechie's up in Chicago with Menace," ManMan replied. "Menace came up on a lick and took Geechie with him to pull it off." There was a moment of silence.

"That dumb nigga makes me so fucking sick!" Cecil snapped. "I told his ass to lay low because Lee was going to come through for me. Patience is a virtue, and it takes patience in order to climb your way back up to the top."

"I heard the take is lovely from Menace. He got about four other dudes to go along with them too. He said the dude was a heavy hitter on the southside of Chicago, but he didn't go into any details with me," ManMan explained.

"Well, what I need for you to do is square that business up with Lay. Give her back the earrings, and try to smooth things over with her. I still want you to try to get on her good side because I'm going to need someone on the inside to find out what Lee's doing."

"A'ight, Cecil, but I'm telling you she don't like me! Byrd told me that she's messing with some tall nigga. Don't nobody seem to know who this cat is but her family."

"I don't give a fuck about some other nigga! I need for you to get close to Lay!" Cecil snapped. "Now if I need to find someone else to do it, then I'll do what I have to."

ManMan held the phone for a minute. "I'll figure something out,

Cecil, man. But I'm telling you that Lay ain't like the average broad. She's got too much of her mama in her," ManMan complained.

"Whatever, ManMan. Get the job done!"

CHAPTER TWENTY-FOUR

"What the fuck are those two up to?" Big Lee hissed.

"What are you talking about?" asked Whisper, walking up behind her. They were standing in the back of the lounge, smoking a blunt, as they watched Lay and Ew Baby get into Lay's car. Both of them were dressed in black skullcaps, black jackets, black leggings, and boots. "Looks like they're about to go handle some business," Whisper replied nonchalantly. Big Lee glared up at Whisper.

"That shit ain't funny," Big Lee fussed. "My baby was pissed off at ManMan, and I want to know what the fuck for."

Whisper looked down at Big Lee and sighed. "I promised Lay that I wasn't going to tell you, but seeing as things are about to get out of hand, I'll tell you what's going on, only if you promise not to get mad," Whisper offered.

"Only if I promise not to get mad? Nigga, you better tell me what's going on with my baby before I take my anger out on you!" Big Lee snapped.

"You betta calm yourself down, Ann!" Whisper snapped. "I ain't none of these other niggas out here! I'll fuck you up back here, talking to me like I'm a kid or something!"

Big Lee stared at Whisper with a hard frown on her face. A part of her wanted to grab him and rip his clothes off because she instantly got aroused when he came at her with all of the aggression. However, she did come to him the wrong way, so Whisper had a valid point.

"Boy, fuck you! You ain't gon' do shit to me!" Big Lee seethed. "Now either you're going to tell me what's going on, or I'm gon' go find out on my own."

Whisper glared at Big Lee because she really pissed him off. "Lay had pawned her earrings to ManMan for Ew Baby," Whisper explained.

"What!" Big Lee shouted.

"Yeah! It was about a month ago. Ew Baby was hot at the crap game and ran out of money. Lay said the dudes from the tracks ran the price up, so Ew Baby needed a little more money to get in the game. They went and hollered at ManMan and pawned the earrings to him. Somehow, he fixed the game and made Ew Baby crap out on her second roll."

"I told them not to be up in there!" Big Lee yelled. "Them hoes are hard headed!"

"I wonder where they get it from, but I tell you one thing." Whisper sighed. "Lay is a grown woman, and you can't run to her rescue every time something happens. She has to learn from her mistakes and grow from them. I know it's hard for her and Ew Baby, living in your shadow, Ann. I have the utmost confidence in Lay, and she'll handle the situation like a mature adult."

"Nigga! She was dressed in all black… You know what she's going to go do if her and Ew Baby are dressed like that." Big Lee scoffed.

Whisper looked at Big Lee for a moment. "I think we need to run around the corner," Whisper uttered.

"I think we need to, too!" Big Lee agreed, and they urgently rushed back into the bar.

****

Lay and Ew Baby walked up in ManMan's place with one goal in mind. Lay was going to get her earrings, or ManMan was going to get fucked up tonight! They headed toward the steps when Big Daddy stopped them mid stride. He looked both of them up and down and noticed their all-black attire. ManMan told him what Lay had done earlier, so he knew they were on some bullshit.

"Where y'all think y'all going?" Big Daddy asked with a smirk on his face. "I need to check y'all."

"You ain't checkin' shit!" spat Ew Baby, frowning. "So move the fuck out of our way!"

Big Daddy frowned back at Ew Baby. "For some reason, your little ass think you tough or something," Big Daddy seethed. "You ain't gon' do shit, Ew Baby, so go sit the fuck down!"

"Bitch ass nigga, try me," Ew Baby spat back. Lay touched Ew Baby's arm and looked at her with a serious expression on her face.

"We ain't come to argue with you, fat man. Move the fuck out of my way, or I'm going to gut your big ass, Shamu," Lay uttered, calmly. She pulled out her switchblade and flicked out the blade. She still had one hand in her pocket, so he knew there had to be a burner in it.

"I ain't got no problems with you ladies," Big Daddy stuttered, throwing up his hands. "I'm just doing my job!"

"I understand, but you need to move the fuck out of my way," Lay demanded. Big Daddy moved over to the side and let the ladies up the steps. Ew Baby jumped at Big Daddy, and he flinched as she laughed. It wasn't that Big Daddy was scared of Lay necessarily. However, he knew that if he got into a confrontation with her, he would have to face her mama and uncles.

Lay and Ew Baby walked to the top of the steps and stared down the hallway. They weren't sure which room ManMan was in, but they were going to check all of them until they found him. Lay slowly walked down the hallway and came to the first door. It was partially cracked, so she pushed it a little to see who was in it. She noticed Shakey sitting in a chair and Byrd approaching her. The pit of Lay's stomach dropped because she couldn't stand the fact that he was messing with Shakey. There was a smug smirk on Shakey's face as Byrd walked up on her. He leaned down and whispered something in Shakey's ear, and she smiled at him coyly. She looked down then reached for Byrd's pants, and Lay wanted to rush inside of the room. Her body wanted to walk away, but for some reason, she just couldn't. She was paralyzed in that spot as she watched Shakey pull down Byrd's pants and start giving him some head.

"What's up," whispered Ew Baby. "Is that nigga in there?"

"No," Lay replied with a lump in her throat. "Let's go!" Lay walked away from the door and started off down the hall. Ew Baby's nosy ass looked through the crack and saw what made Lay walk away so quickly.

"Nasty bitch!" Ew Baby called out. Byrd quickly turned around, but Ew Baby was gone before he could see who it was. He looked down as Shakey and smiled because he recognized Ew Baby's voice. He knew that she would go back and tell Lay, but what he didn't know was that Lay had already seen it with her own eyes.

The women came up on a back bedroom and figured ManMan was probably in there. Lay knocked on the door, and ManMan summoned them to come inside. Lay turned the doorknob, and ManMan was sitting on a bed with a smile on his face. Lay came partially into the room but stopped when she noticed a girl sitting in a chair next to the window.

"I was expecting you," ManMan smiled. "Big Daddy told me you were on your way up."

"So you should have my shit ready," Lay retorted. She reached into her pocket and pulled out a roll of money. She threw it at ManMan and stared as Ew Baby stood on the side of her.

"Daaaamn. They look like they came to do damage." The girl sitting in the room laughed. ManMan looked over at her crossly then back at the women.

"You can count it, but it's all there," Lay assured him.

"Did you include the money for my windows?" ManMan scoffed.

"Naw. But I got 6 shots you can have for them muthafuckas," Lay retorted. "Give me my shit so I can get the fuck up out of here!"

"Aye, go back downstairs, baby, and I'll come and get you in a few minutes," ManMan instructed.

"Okay, ManMan." The girl smiled. She got up out of the chair and walked past the women. Lay glared at her as she passed, but Ew Baby was all up in her grill.

"You won't give me no play, but you gon' have that tired ass trick up in here?" Ew Baby hissed and frowned. The girl giggled as she walked down the hall because she couldn't believe what she was hearing.

"Ew Baby, be quiet." Lay scoffed. "Come on, ManMan. I don't have all day. Give me my earrings so we both can be out of each other's hair."

"Maybe I like being in your hair, Lay," ManMan mocked. He got up and walked over to his closet and went inside of it. Lay adjusted herself in order to watch him because she didn't trust this muthafucka as far as she could throw him. He reached up on the shelf and grabbed a shoebox. Next, he walked toward her with it and held it out in front of him.

"What the fuck is this?" Lay snapped.

"Open it up, Lay," ManMan instructed. Lay looked up at ManMan before she opened the box. Her earrings were sitting inside of it, along with a small jewelry box. She reached inside and grabbed her earrings because this ordeal was finally over!

"Thank you," Lay said dryly.

"Now are we cool?" asked ManMan curiously.

"Copasetic," Lay replied smugly. She turned to walk away, but ManMan put his hand on her shoulder.

"Wait a minute, Lay," ManMan called out. "I want to apologize for being such a dick. I thought maybe if I held out on giving you your earrings, you would give me a chance to go out with you. I see now that it was stupid, and I want to say I'm sorry."

Lay looked at his hand then back up at him. "It's cool, ManMan, but I keep telling you that I'm not interested," Lay replied. "I forgive you, but don't ever cross me again!"

"I've learned my lesson," ManMan admitted. "Let's go downstairs and have a drink."

"That sounds excellent!" Ew Baby interjected.

"I'm ready to go," Lay replied smugly.

"One little drink ain't gon' hurt nothing!" Ew Baby protested. Lay side eyed Ew Baby because she knew why Ew Baby wanted to stay. Whenever they walked into the gambling house, she was always ready to shoot.

"Okay, Ew Baby, but I ain't gon' be in here all night," Lay fussed.

"Great, ladies!" ManMan beamed. "Let's go downstairs."

CHAPTER TWENTY-FIVE

One Month Later

Big Lee was standing at the window and noticed Amber leaving Whisper's house. She watched as Whisper walked out behind her and stood on the sidewalk. He had a frustrated look on his face, so she wondered what that was about. She was under the impression that things were over between them, so what could she have possibly wanted?

Whisper walked up to the door and came into Big Lee's house. She was sitting on the couch, smoking a blunt as he made his way into the living room. Big Lee wanted to ask him why was Amber at his house, but she decided against it. The way he slumped down on the couch, she knew that something was up with him.

"What's wrong with you?" asked Big Lee, handing Whisper the blunt.

"Amber just left my house with some bullshit." Whisper sighed. He hit the blunt a few times then passed it back.

"What kind of bullshit?" Big Lee asked curiously. She hit the blunt and tried to be nonchalant about it, but the anticipation was getting the best of her. She wanted to know what was going on, like yesterday.

"Before I tell you, I want to ask you something," Whisper replied.

"Is it something that's going to piss me off?" asked Big Lee. "Because I'm not in the mood for no bullshit, Whisper."

He smiled at Big Lee and took the blunt from her. "Look at you! Ready to start going off already." He laughed. "What I wanted to know is"—Whisper looked at Big Lee, sincerely—"I want to know if we're ever going to get married? I know we brushed over the subject last month, but I want to know if we're actually going to be together as husband and wife, or are we going to keep shacking up?"

"Does this have something to do with your little visit?" asked Big Lee frankly. "I saw Ms. Thing leaving your house a few minutes ago."

"You were spying on me?" asked Whisper.

"No! I was looking out of the window and saw her walking to her car," Big Lee explained. "You know I'm always in the window, so naturally, I saw her while I was doing my checks."

Whisper put the blunt roach in the ashtray and sat back on the couch. "Can you just answer the question, Ann, please?" Whisper asked with a moan. Big Lee smiled at Whisper and got up off the couch. She walked over and sat down next to him on the loveseat.

"Okay, Whisper, let's talk turkey." Big Lee sighed. "You know I love you and—"

"Here you go, Ann, with that bullshit! Please don't try to carry me, because I need an honest answer from you!" Whisper fussed. "This bitch just told me that she's pregnant, and I need to know if I'm waiting on you in vain." Big Lee's eyes widened as she leaned back in shock.

"Amber's pregnant?" asked Big Lee.

"That's what she said," Whisper replied solemnly. "I mean, I care about Amber, but I love you, Ann. You know I've always wanted to be with you, but you and Cecil's situation seemed to be the one thing holding us up."

"I'm at a loss for words, Whisper," Big Lee admitted. "I mean, there's no situation with me and Cecil, because I told you that we're no longer married. I told you that a while ago, so that has nothing to do with nothing."

"But you haven't told him yet," Whisper replied. "And that has something to do with everything." Big Lee looked at Whisper, and for the first time, she saw how vulnerable he was feeling. "Ann, I want to marry you, and I'm asking you—right here, right now—if you want my last name." Big Lee sat back on the couch with a perplexed look on her face. She didn't know what to do, because she knew the day would come when Whisper would ask her to be with him, but marriage. Big Lee hated Amber, and she knew that it was going to be problems if she were pregnant by Whisper, but was that a big enough reason not to be with him? "Can you answer my question? The silence is killing me right now!" Big Lee took Whisper's hand and stared into his eyes deeply.

"I say…" Big Lee leaned forward and grabbed Whisper's face. She looked into his eyes and saw the urgency for her response.

"You're about to say that we need to wait!" Whisper blurted out. He jumped up out of his seat and stared down at Big Lee angrily. "You always put other people before me, Ann, and that really hurts!" Big Lee looked at Whisper and jumped to her feet.

"Nigga! Shut the fuck up and listen to what I have to say!" Big Lee yelled. "What I was about to say to you before you so rudely interrupted me was"—she pushed him with both hands against his chest—"I want to make this official with us. I'm sorry that I made you wait so long, but I can no longer deny the fact that we're already together. I don't rock with no other niggas, and you know that. I accepted Amber being with you because I felt it wouldn't be fair to ask you not to mess with other people because of the Cecil situation. However, I could give a fuck less about that bitch being pregnant. We're going to take care of that baby like we take care of all of our babies. I love you, Whisper, and I'm ready to be all of yours—mind, body and soul."

Whisper stared at Big Lee in shock because he couldn't believe what he just heard. "You're serious, right? You're not just jerking my chain?" asked Whisper. Big Lee grabbed his hand and pulled him close to her. She wrapped her arms around his waist and stared up at him lovingly.

"I'm serious as a heart attack," Big Lee declared. "Now give me a kiss before I change my mind!" Whisper leaned down and kissed Big Lee on the lips. He pulled away and stared at her for a second then leaned down for another kiss. He pressed his lips firmly against hers and swept his tongue in her mouth. He slid his hands down her body and gripped her ass firmly. Big Lee reached down and unfastened

Whisper's pants because this caused for a celebration. She eased her hand into his boxers and massaged his manhood while they continued to kiss lustfully. Big Lee pulled away and stared at Whisper coyly. "We better lock the door before somebody decides to walk in on us."

"That's a good idea!" Whisper agreed. "Let me go handle that!"

Big Lee slid her dress down her shoulders and let it hit the floor while Whisper went to lock the door. He turned and smiled as he saw the love of his life waiting for him naked. He slid his coat off and threw it on the floor. Next, he pulled his sweatshirt and t-shirt off, throwing them down as well. He walked up on her and put both of his hands against her large breasts.

He was happy that Big Lee decided that she was willing to look over the fact that Amber was pregnant. He felt like Amber was lying because she realized how much she'd lose when Whisper cut her off. He wanted to get a paternity test when the baby was born because he needed hardcore facts instead of taking the word of a scorned lover. This was a triumphant day for Whisper because now he no longer had to hide the fact that Big Lee was his woman, and he damn sure was going to make everyone know that things were official between the two of them.

Lay pulled up at the Mobile station to grab a pack of blunts. She'd been rocking with Reed for the past few weeks, but she still missed Byrd. They hadn't spoken since the night they'd gotten into the argument, but after she saw the episode with him and Shakey, she felt like things were basically over between them.

Lay got out of her car and went into the store. Shakey was

standing at the counter and noticed Lay when she walked in. Shakey couldn't stand Lay because she knew about her relationship with Byrd. Byrd had told her a while ago that he was messing with Lay and that things between them were getting serious. So when Byrd came at her and asked if she had a man, Shakey was confused because she thought he and Lay were rocking together. However, when he fucked her on the first night, she figured that things weren't quite what they seemed.

Lay walked up in line and waited to be helped. Shakey grabbed her stuff off the counter then turned to leave the store. She made sure that she walked past Lay and bumped her hard when she went passed.

"Uhhh, excuse you." Lay scoffed. "Ole rude bitch!"

"What you say?" Shakey snapped. "'Cause I smack bitches!"

"Well if you see a bitch, come smack a bitch!" Lay retorted. Shakey looked at Lay and laughed.

"Girl, fuck you! You just mad 'cause Byrd don't want your ass no more," Shakey hissed. She turned to walk out of the store but not before she said one more thing. "It's obvious that you're bitter, and the way I see it"—Shakey smacked her lips then flipped her braids over her shoulder—"you are the weakest link. Goodbye!" Shakey walked out of the store while the other customers laughed and commented about the exchange. Lay was stewing by this point, and she refused to let the shit go.

Lay came out of the store and walked to her car. She noticed Shakey leaning against Byrd's car, but she didn't see him anywhere around. She opened her door and placed her purse and bag on the seat. She put her key fold inside of her pocket and shut the door quickly.

She was going to see just how tough this bitch actually was since she wanted to pretend like she was about that life.

Lay walked up on Shakey and stood in front of her. She slapped the shit out of Shakey, causing her to drop her drink on the ground. Shakey held her cheek as she stared at Lay in disbelief.

"What was that shit you were just talking inside of there?" Lay spat. "You want to play pussy, bitch, so now you're about to get fucked!"

"I ain't no punk!" shouted Shakey, and she swung, connecting a punch to Lay's face. Lay stepped back and started whaling punches in a rapid speed against Shakey's face. She grabbed Shakey by her long braids, wrapping them around her hand in one smooth motion. She pulled Shakey's head down and started sending uppercuts to her face while Shakey screamed out in pain. All of a sudden, Lay felt someone grab her from behind, but she refused to let Shakey go because she didn't know if it was one of Shakey's girls grabbing her.

"Let her go, Lay!" Byrd shouted.

"I ain't letting this bitch go until you let me go!" Lay retorted. She hit Shakey a few more times while Byrd tried to pull Lay off of her. He continued to pull Lay backward, and she held on to Shakey, pulling her right along with them.

"This bitch got my hair, bae! Make her let me go!" Shakey shouted.

"Yeah, bae!" Lay mocked. "Make me let your bitch go!"

"Come on, Lay! You're being childish! You done already got your shit off, so let her go!" Byrd demanded. Lay let Shakey's hair go, and she and Byrd went back a few steps. Shakey touched her nose and felt blood, sending her into hysterical screams. She ran toward Lay and started swinging, connecting any punch that she could.

"So you gon' hold me so that this bitch can hit me!" Lay shouted in disbelief. She lifted her foot and booted Shakey in the stomach, sending her flying backward on the ground. Lay reached into her pocket and pulled out her switchblade. She flicked it open and jabbed it into Byrd's leg, twisting it around in a circle.

"Ah, shit, Lay!" Byrd screamed out in pain. "You just stabbed me!" He let Lay go as she turned to face him.

"You damn right, bitch ass nigga, because as far as I'm concerned, y'all jumped me!" Lay spat. She stared at him vehemently because she couldn't believe it herself. Never in a million years did she think Byrd would help some bitch fight her!

"You know it wasn't shit like that!" Byrd retorted. "You were wrong as fuck!" Lay pulled her knife out of his leg and stared at him, unbothered by his words.

"Fuck both of y'all!" Lay spat. She wiped her knife off on his coat then turned and walked away. She jumped in her car and backed back, but she blew at Byrd before she pulled off the lot. Her mama's name was Big Lee, and she taught her daughter to fuck up anyone who opposed her, so they got what was coming to them!

CHAPTER TWENTY-SIX

Lay was messed up about what happened after her adrenaline came down. She instantly went to the lounge to tell her mama about the events that had occurred. Big Lee had already gotten a phone call from someone, telling her that Lay was up at the gas station fighting. By the time Whisper had made it up there, Lay was in her car, pulling off the lot. Whisper went to see what had happened, and Byrd explained that Lay and Shakey were fighting. He told Whisper that he had grabbed Lay because she had already beaten Shakey up, but when Lay let Shakey go, she ran up and hit Lay a few times. This must have pissed Lay off because then she pulled out a knife and stabbed Byrd in the leg. Byrd was bleeding pretty badly, and Whisper urged him to go to the hospital.

Tabitha called Big Lee shortly after and told her that Byrd needed to get some stitches. She wanted to know why Lay did that to her son, and Big Lee explained the situation. She wasn't happy, but she told Big Lee that Lay was out of line. Big Lee said her baby felt threatened, so she acted accordingly, and Byrd should have never grabbed Lay in the first place, she conveyed. Needless to say, both mothers were pissed about the entire situation, but they were both going to ride on the side of their child.

Lay was sitting at the bar, sipping on Don Julio straight. She had been there since around 5:00 p.m., and it was just a little past 11:00 p.m. Ew Baby worked Lay's shift behind the bar and wished she had been there to help her sister fight.

"You know if I was there, we would have tore some shit up!" Ew Baby signified.

"I know, sis," Lay slurred. "They both had me fucked up! But I can't believe that I stabbed Byrd. I love him, Ew Baby!"

"I know, sis, but fuck that shit! I would have stabbed that nigga too if he would have done some hip shit like that! I bet he'll think twice before he run up to help another bitch!" Ew Baby insisted and laughed. "I heard he had to get about thirty stitches."

Lay looked up at Ew Baby sadly then held her head down.

"But why do I feel so bad?" asked Lay, confused. "I never wanted to hurt him. I just wanted him to let me go! Why did he have to help that bitch?"

"Because that's what niggas do when they see their girlfriends getting their asses kicked," Big Lee interjected forcefully. She walked up on Lay and rubbed her back. She knew her baby was hurting already because she and Byrd weren't together. However, now that she'd stabbed him, the chances of them getting together were really over. "I think you need to stop drinking and go home, baby."

"I don't want to go home, Mama," Lay whined. "I just want to go see if Byrd is alright."

"The last thing you need to do is go see that boy," Big Lee insisted. "He'd probably try to smack fire from your ass!" Big Lee laughed as Ew Baby smiled at her mother.

"Mama, it's not funny!" Lay cried. "He's going to hate me forever, and I'll never marry him now!" Tears formed in Lay's eyes as she knocked down the rest of her drink. "I'm just going to stay here on this stool until Byrd forgives me," Lay cried. Big Lee handed her a napkin and watched as Lay let the tears flow and wallowed in sorrow.

****

Byrd was sitting on his couch, watching television. Shakey was in the kitchen, fixing him something to eat because they'd just come from the hospital. He wasn't sure why the fight had occurred, but he never imagined that Lay would take things this far. His feelings were hurt that Lay would do something like this to him. All he ever wanted was for them to be together, but after today, he didn't know if he could forgive her.

"You want me to bring you your food, or do you want to eat in the kitchen?" Shakey called out. Byrd didn't answer, because he was deep in thought. Shakey came out of the kitchen and walked up to the couch. "Byrd! Did you hear me?"

He turned and looked at her with a frown on his face. "Naw, I ain't hear you," he replied. "What did you say?"

"I asked if you wanted me to bring your dinner to you?" Shakey huffed. She put her hands on her hips as she stared at him, annoyed.

"I ain't hungry, man," Byrd replied, sounding agitated.

"What! I wish I would have known that before I heated up that food." She scoffed.

Byrd glared at Shakey as he narrowed his eyes at her. "All you did was heat up a microwave dinner." He scoffed. "It ain't like you actually did something!"

Shakey looked at Byrd strangely. "I don't know why you got an attitude with me," Shakey fussed. "I ain't the bitch who stabbed you!"

"Bitch, no you didn't just say that shit to me! Your dusty ass is the reason I got stabbed in the first place!" Byrd snapped. "And since we're on the subject, why were you fighting anyway?"

Shakey looked at Byrd blankly. "I don't know why that bitch ran up on me," Shakey lied. "I guess she's just jealous because we're together." Byrd stared at Shakey accusingly because he knew that Lay wasn't petty like that. Even if Lay was tripping off of them being together, she would keep her distance instead of starting a fight. "Why you looking at me like that? I know you're not going to take her side on the situation. That's why she stabbed you; because she's mad that we're together!"

"I guess," Byrd replied. "Can you go get me a glass of water so I can take a few of these pain pills?" A smile came across Shakey's face.

"Okay, bae," she replied happily. Shakey left to go get Byrd's water when his text message signal went off. He grabbed his phone and saw a text from Lay. His stomach dropped when he saw her name, and he wondered what could she possibly want after she stabbed him in the leg. He wasn't going to look at the message at first, but his curiosity was too piqued not to look.

Text Message: *I'm soooo sorry for what I did to you! My heart is heavy, and I feel so bad about it! I LOVE YOU BYRD, and I WOULD NEVER WANT TO HURT YOU! I HOPE YOU CAN FIND IT IN YOUR HEART TO FORGIVE ME!!!! BUT IF YOU CAN'T… I UNDERSTAND. I MEAN IT WHEN I SAY I LOVE YOU because I TRULY DO! I*

FUCKED UP and AGAIN I AM SOOOO SORRY!!!!

Byrd stared at his phone while tears formed in his eyes. He was angry at Lay and couldn't believe that she would have the nerve to text him with an apology. Why didn't she call him or come to see if he was alright? A text message didn't mean shit in his eyes. If she were truly sorry and cared, she would have been right there with him at the hospital.

Shakey came back into the room and noticed the tear stains on Byrd's cheeks. He quickly put his phone down and wiped his face as Shakey handed him the glass of water. She was curious to why Byrd was crying and why he quickly put down his phone.

"What's the matter, bae?" asked Shakey nosily.

"Nothing," Byrd mumbled. "I'm just in a lot of pain."

"Are you sure you're in pain, or does it have something to do with the text message you just received?" Shakey turned up her lips and crossed her arms in front of her.

"Bitch, who are you? The got damn detectives?" Byrd snapped. "I told you that I'm in pain! So quit asking me a bunch of stupid ass questions, because you're starting to piss me off!"

"Why you getting an attitude with me! I ain't did shit to you!" Shakey hissed. "See, I ain't about to be bothered with this shit! I'm about to call my homegirl so she can come swoop me up!"

"So that's how you gon' play shit?" Byrd seethed. He pulled himself up off the couch. "Get your shit and get the fuck out of my house! You can call that bitch from the lobby!"

Shakey looked at him in disbelief. "You're putting me out!" she stammered.

"You damn right!" he shouted. "Now grab your shit!" A frown came across Shakey's face as she stormed over to his table. She grabbed her coat and purse then charged over to the door.

"Fuck you, Byrd! I don't need this shit!" shouted Shakey. She opened his door and slammed it hard behind herself while Byrd stood staring at it vehemently.

****

Lay stumbled out of the lounge with Whisper following up behind her. She was three shades to the west and felt like the weight of the world was on her shoulders. She kept crying about how much she loved Byrd and how if she could take it back, she would. Whisper told her to give it time, and hopefully, Byrd would eventually forgive her. Lay felt like Byrd wasn't going to forgive her and that her life was over at this point.

Whisper walked Lay home and took her in the house. He walked her to the couch and took off her coat. He made her sit down because she kept swaying back and forth. Next, he sat beside her and pushed her back to take off her shoes. She stared at him dreamily as she watched him care for her.

"Why can't we be together, Whisper?" slurred Lay. "You're always looking out for me, and you love me, don't you?" Whisper laughed at Lay because he knew she was drunk.

"You're talking crazy, little girl," Whisper replied and laughed. "You know I'm in love with your mama, and besides, you're my goddaughter."

"I know you love my mama, but she don't do you right. She treats your relationship like a dirty little secret, and I wouldn't do that to you. Well, I did that to Byrd, and that's why we're not together, but I would love you and would take good care of you! Don't you think I'm beautiful?"

"Of course, I think you're beautiful, but that ain't for us, Lay. I look at you as my daughter, and if your mama found out that we were messing around, she would definitely kill me," Whisper replied.

"But I love you, Whisper," Lay declared. She sat up and wrapped her arms around Whisper's neck and tried to kiss him.

"Hold the fuck up, Lay! What are you doing?" Whisper snapped. Lay looked at him like a deer in headlights.

"I'm sorry, Whisper," she sobbed. "I just keep fucking up!" She buried her face in his chest as the tears flowed like a faucet. "I just want to be loved."

"Ah, baby girl..." Whisper sighed as he wrapped his arms around her. "Don't cry, Lay. Things are going to be alright." She pulled away and stared at him, frightened.

"Please don't tell my mama," she sobbed. "I don't want her mad at me for trying to kiss you."

"It's cool, Lay. I won't tell if you don't," he bargained. "Now lay back and get some sleep 'cause your ass is drunk and tripping!" Lay fell back and wiped her eyes. Whisper grabbed a blanket that sat on the back of the couch and covered her up. He started to wonder about what Deacon had said to him about Lay being his daughter. He needed to confront Big Lee about the situation because he couldn't have Lay coming on to him like that. It would be fucked up if Lay were actually his daughter. Why would Ann not tell him? It just didn't make any sense. Lay sat up and turned to the side. She started to vomit all over the floor while Whisper sat feeling confused.

"I don't feel so good…" Lay moaned, dry heaving.

"A drunk ain't shit!" Whisper yelled. Then he reached over and rubbed Lay's back as she continued to throw up some more. "Your godfather got you, baby girl. Don't you worry!"

CHAPTER TWENTY-SEVEN

Geechie stood at the door of the garage, feeling antsy. He was meeting up with Cam and Ax to get his monthly package from them. Big Lee decided to throw Cecil a play for the next couple of months until he got out of prison. Since she was going to tell him the truth about their marriage when he got out, she felt that being nice to him would soften the blow. Cam came to the door and opened it for Geechie. He watched as Geechie stumbled into the garage, high as a test pilot. He looked outside the door and noticed a couple of Geechie's cronies standing outside, waiting. He didn't like the looks of it, because normally, Geechie was by himself.

"What's up with those niggas standing outside the door?" Cam asked with a frown on his face.

"Ah, don't trip off of them," Geechie stuttered. "They're just waiting for me since I'm picking up such a large package. I wanted to have somebody here to watch my back."

"Ain't nobody gon' do shit to you, nigga!" Cam huffed. Geechie looked back at Cam smugly then walked over to where Ax was standing.

"You got our money?" asked Ax sternly.

"Don't ask me no dumb ass questions," Geechie hissed, throwing the duffle bag at Ax's feet. Ax looked down at the bag then back up at Geechie.

"Don't be throwing shit at me like I'm a damn dog or something!" Ax snapped. "You ain't beyond getting fucked up, Geechie!" Geechie laughed as he looked back at Cam.

"Y'all niggas kills me!" Geechie declared and laughed. "Since Big Lee's been on, you niggas act like some real pussies!"

"Naw, you and your brother are some pussies!" Ax seethed. "I heard that nigga Cecil's the one who likes to take it up the ass!" Ax started laughing, and Cam joined in.

"Your brother's a fuck boy!" Cam added as they continued to laugh heartily.

"What the fuck did you just say to me?" Geechie snapped with an evil grimace on his face. "Boy, I'll fuck both of you niggas up right now!"

"You ain't gon' do shit here, patna!" Ax hissed. "You know how we get down, Geechie. You don't want no smoke!" Ax raised his shirt, showing the handle of his gun.

"You ain't the only nigga that got heat," Geechie seethed. "Now give me my shit so I can get the fuck out of here!"

"Give that nigga his shit," Cam called out and laughed. "This bitch ass nigga is all in his feelings."

"Whatever," Geechie scoffed. Ax walked over to a car that was sitting in the garage. He opened the door and pulled out a box that read: Auto Parts. Next, he carried it over to Geechie and dropped it at his feet.

"Open it up, and make sure it's what you asked for," Ax instructed. He leaned down and picked up the duffle bag of money and carried it over to the table. He unzipped it and started pulling out the stacks of cash. Geechie opened the box and smiled because this was more dope than he was used to seeing. Big Lee had delivered just like Cecil promised, but as far as Geechie was concerned, she should have given the dope to Cecil for free.

"It's all here," said Geechie, closing up the box. He stood up with the box in his hands and stared vehemently at Ax while he counted the money.

"All the money is here, so you can leave," Ax replied. He never turned around to face Geechie, and Geechie took that as a sign as disrespect.

"So you gon' keep your back to me, nigga?" asked Geechie with an attitude.

"What I got to face you for?" Ax asked frankly. "You got your shit, so leave!"

"Yeah, a'ight, nigga," Geechie seethed. He turned and started toward the door as Cam stared at him smugly.

"Next time you better come with a better disposition, ole bitch ass nigga," said Cam arrogantly. "Or next time, you won't be getting shit!"

"Whatever, soft ass nigga," Geechie retorted. Cam smiled smugly at Geechie as he opened the door. Cam noticed that the two men were no longer standing outside the door, and they were nowhere in sight.

"It looks like your mans and nem left you, Geechie," Cam teased. Geechie walked out of the door, and Cam closed it behind him. "Can you believe that nigga?" Cam walked away from the door and headed toward Ax. He forgot to lock the handle behind him, and all of a sudden, the door flew open. three niggas rushed in with ski masks on and their guns drawn.

"Put your fucking hands up!" shouted one of the men. Cam stopped in his tracks and looked over at Ax. He quickly turned around with his gun in hand and started firing shots in the men's direction. Ax turned around with a chopper in his hand and pointed it toward the men. One of the men started firing back, while the other two ducked down for cover.

Cam tried to run backward to get out of the way when several of the shots hit him in the chest. He fell to floor as the men started rushing toward Ax. Ax ducked down behind a car and flipped the clip over. He pulled the pen back, jumped up, and then started firing off rounds. The man that was in the front fell to the ground as the other two ran back toward the door. Ax started walking toward them as he continued to unload the clip from his riffle. He clipped one of the men as they tried to run out of the door, and he heard Geechie yell for them to get in the car as he made it to the door. Ax stepped out of the door and started firing shots at the car as it rode off. Whisper ran out in the middle of the street and started firing at the car as well. Big Lee ran across the street toward the garage as Deacon came running down the street.

"Where is Cam?" Big Lee shouted.

"He's in the shop!" yelled Ax anxiously. "And he's hurt pretty badly!"

"Oh my God!" Big Lee cried, running in the shop. She saw Cam lying on the floor in a puddle of blood. She rushed over to him as panic rose up in her. "Call an ambulance! Somebody call an ambulance!" Deacon ran into the shop and saw Cam lying on the floor. He reached into his pocket and pulled out his phone. "Cam! Cam, can you hear me?"

"I'm cool, big sis." Cam coughed. "I got hit a few times, but they ain't do no damage." Whisper ran up in the shop along with Ax, Ralph, and Rico.

"Lock that door," Deacon instructed. He talked to the dispatch and told them to send an ambulance. "The police will be here in a few minutes, so we have to act fast." Whisper walked over to the man rolling around on the floor. He bent down and pulled off his ski mask and noticed it was one of Geechie's little cronies.

"Aye, Whisper, man, don't hurt me," begged the man. "I'm already shot pretty bad!"

"Nigga, so!" retorted Whisper before he let off a few rounds in the man's head.

"Damn, Whisper!" shouted Deacon. "Now we got to get rid of a body!" Whisper looked up at Deacon with no remorse.

"Maaaan, fuck this nigga! Is my bro gon' be alright?" Whisper questioned.

"He'll be okay if the damn ambulance would come on!" Big Lee sobbed. "Please hold on, Cam. It's going to be okay." Cam looked at his sister and smiled.

"I know, Big Lee," he mumbled. Cam started coughing profusely as blood splattered out of his mouth.

"Call them muthafuckas back, Deacon!" Big Lee cried in a panic. "Call them now!" Cam looked up at Big Lee and gasped for air.

"I love y'all," Cam uttered, then his head fell off to the side.

"Cam!" shouted Big Lee. "Cameron!" She collapsed on top of his body as tears poured down her face. "Nooooo! Noooo!" she screamed as Ax ran over to them. Ralph had taken the chopper from Ax and went to put it away in the office, and Rico had started getting stuff to wrap up the dead body of the robber. They stopped in their tracks and ran over to Cam.

"Killa Cam!" Ax yelled urgently. "Wake the fuck up!" He dropped to his knees next to his brother. "Please wake up, bro!" Deacon walked over to them and fell to his knees.

"God, please watch over my brother's soul. He wasn't no bad guy, and I hope you are merciful in your judgment toward him," Deacon cried. Big Lee laid her head down on top of Cam and let out a gut-wrenching scream. There was some beating on the door, and no one moved. Whisper had wrapped the dead body up in a tarp and dragged it over in the corner of the shop. There were some random car parts sitting next to where he'd put the body, so he decided to cover it up with them.

"Get the door!" Deacon yelled out. Whisper looked back at them then headed over toward the door. He opened it up, and Craig pushed his way inside. Lay came behind him, and as soon as she saw her mother draped over Cam, she instantly started screaming.

"Get Lay the fuck out of here!" Deacon ordered.

"Is he dead?" Lay stammered as tears poured down her cheeks. "Whisper, is Cam dead?"

"I'm sorry, baby girl," Whisper crooned. Lay buried her face in Whisper's chest as she grabbed ahold of his jacket.

"Why did they kill him?" cried Lay. "Why, Whisper? Why?" Whisper wrapped his arms around Lay as the ambulance pulled up in front of the garage. They rushed in as all of Cam's siblings surrounded him. Big Lee was the most distraught between all of them, and she fought her brothers as they pulled her off of Cam. She continued to scream and yell as they dragged her out of the garage. It was a sad day for the Wilson Family because this was a major loss for all of them!

TO BE CONTINUED…

ACKNOWLEDGEMENTS

I would like to Thank God for giving me this gift of writing. It is a blessing to be able to share my stories with you guys, and I appreciate each and every one of you that come along on my adventures! I would like to thank my publisher, Porscha Sterling, for believing in me and giving me the opportunity to put my thoughts out here in the world!! I am truly grateful to you and the Royalty Publishing House Family for all of your love and support!! I would like to give a special shout out to Quiana Nicole and Michelle Davis for all of her help and support!! I've come to understand that you are a major gear in this crazy machine that keeps us shining, and I want you to know that I appreciate you! (XoXo). I can't forget my AWESOME editor, Latisha Smith Burns, and her editing team at Touch of Class Publishing Services: "Where class meets perfection!" You are truly a gem, and I appreciate all of the love and support that you give me!! You get my oddness, and I am so grateful that you do!! To my test reader, LaShonda "Shawny" Jennings, thank you for your input and "realness"! You give me my reality check, and I appreciate the love and support!! I am thankful that you are a part of my literary career because you keep me focused!! To my readers, THANK YOU! THANK YOU!! THANK YOU!!! YOU GUYS ARE ROCK STARS, and I AM TRULY GRATEFUL TO YOU!! YOU'RE THE REAL MVP'S!!!!!!!!

PEACE, LOVE, & BLESSINGS

Vivian Blue

CHECK ME OUT ON SOCIAL MEDIA

Facebook: Vivian Blue

Instagram: Authorvivianblue

Twitter: @VivBlueAuthor

My website: http://www.Vivianblueauthor.com

Amazon Author's Page: http://www.amzn.com/-/e/B0177JADR6

Facebook Likes Page:

http://www.Facebook.com/Vivian-Blue-3889021813110701

BOOK TITLES

**Torn Between Two Bosses: The Series*

**Rise of a Kingpin's Wife: The Series, with a follow up: Forever A Kingpin's Wife: The Series*

**A West Side Love Story: The Series*

**Gangsta: A Colombian Cartel Love Story: The Series*

**Friends Before Lovers, Standalone*

**Love, Marriage, and Infidelity: The Series*

**They Don't Know About Us: The Series **

**War of the Hearts: The Series*

**She's a Savage for a Real Gangsta: The Series*

My Heart Is in Harmony by V. Marie (young adult) Standalone

Looking for a publishing home?

Royalty Publishing House, Where the Royals reside, is accepting submissions for writers in the urban fiction genre. If you're interested, submit the first 3-4 chapters with your synopsis to submissions@royaltypublishinghouse.com.

Check out our website for more information:

www.royaltypublishinghouse.com.

CPSIA information can be obtained
at www.ICGtesting.com
Printed in the USA
LVHW032205031019
633107LV00013B/287